HOME
FOR THE
HOWL-IDAYS

Also by Dian Curtis Regan:

The Vampire Who Came for Christmas
My Zombie Valentine
Liver Cookies
The Kissing Contest
The Ghost Twins series

HOME
FOR THE
HOWL-IDAYS

DIAN CURTIS REGAN

AN
APPLE
PAPERBACK

SCHOLASTIC INC.
New York Toronto London Auckland Sydney

ISBN 0-590-48772-8

12 11 10 9 8 7 6 5 4 3 2 1   4 5 6 7 8 9/9

Printed in the U.S.A.   40

First Scholastic printing, November 1994

For Brian, Michael, and Laura Winterscheidt

Contents

HOME FOR THE HOWL-DAYS

1.
A Balloon of Doom

Samuel M. Hollister (the third) leaped onto the train the instant the doors slid open. *Free at last!* his mind sang.

Free from boarding school for two whole weeks — no homework, no uniforms, no mandatory participation in sports, and — best of all — no Jake Wise to make life in the sixth grade miserable.

Sam never believed holiday vacations truly started until he stepped onto the train bound for home — the Hollister mansion in the town of Hollister.

Thanks to his famous grandfather, Samuel M. Hollister (the first), inventor of the most popular board game in history (*Run for Your Life*), practically everything in town was named after him.

Humming "Jingle Bells," Sam swung his leather travel bag into an overhead bin, then settled onto a seat, opening a book he'd been eager to read: *The Vampire Who Came for Christmas.*

He loved stories about vampires and zombies and other creatures of the night. It was easy to see why, after growing up playing his grandfather's game, year after year. A game that revolved around monsters.

"Well?" came the scratchy voice that interrupted most of his daydreams. "Aren't you going to help me with my luggage?"

Sighing, Sam stood, taking the bag from his stepsister, Leesha. Aleesha Jane Hollister, the *first*. (She liked to remind everyone *she* was an original, not a copy like her stepbrother.)

Shoving her bag next to his, Sam returned to his seat and book, wishing Leesha would sit in another row so he wouldn't have to listen to her.

"Want to see what I bought everyone for Christmas?" she chirped, opening a huge bag from Dobson's — *the* most expensive store in the mall near Woodhaven, their boarding school.

"Do I have a choice?" Sam closed his book with reluctance while she dug through crinkly tissue paper.

"Nothing is wrapped yet. Emma can do it."

Emma was housekeeper and nanny at the Hollister mansion, but Leesha acted as though Emma was her personal servant. As she did Sam.

"This is for Mummy." Leesha showed him a dove, caught mid-flight in sparkling crystal, a sprig of real holly berries in its beak. "Mummy collects doves, you know."

2

"I know." Sam was also giving a dove to his new mother. (New, because Leesha's mother had recently married his father.) Sam's dove was carved (by him) out of balsa wood. But after seeing Leesha's expensive gift, it made him want to throw *his* out the window of the speeding train.

"Think Mummy will like it?" Leesha gushed.

He nodded, resisting another argument over Leesha's annoying nickname for her mom. It was hard enough for him to say *Mother*, after not having one for eight years. He refused to use a name that sounded so silly.

"This is for Webster." Leesha lifted a book called *The Universe and You* from the shopping bag. Webster was her little brother.

"He can't read that," Sam said. "He's only five."

"He's very smart for his age," Leesha snipped, always quick to defend Web. "And he's going to be an astronomer someday. Or an astronaut."

"How do *you* know?"

"Because he loves books about stars and planets and the moon. Sometimes at night, he stares at the sky for hours."

Sam thought his stepbrother stared out the window because he wasn't too bright. *He'd* bought Web a teddy bear dressed like Elvis.

The train quickly filled with other passengers heading home for the holidays. At each stop, frigid air patted Sam's cheeks when the doors *whooshed* open.

3

Leesha reached into the Dobson bag and pulled out a box wrapped in gold foil. "This is for — "

"I'd rather be surprised by the rest of your gifts on Christmas morning," Sam said, stopping her. Rolling his jacket into a ball, he placed it against the window for a pillow. "Wake me when we get to Hollister."

Sleep had been a rare luxury the past two weeks, thanks to rehearsals for the Christmas pageant. (He played an ox; Leesha was miscast as an angel.)

Then there was the cast and crew party, and receptions for the Debate Club, Environmental Club, and Future Leaders of America, *plus* late-night cramming sessions for end-of-the-quarter tests.

Fidgeting in his seat, Sam tried to find a cozy position for napping. If only he was wearing something more comfortable than his horrid uniform.

Black pants, black shoes, black sports coat, black tie. He *hated* black. When he finished at Woodhaven, he'd *never* wear black again.

A hand shook his shoulder, waking him.

Sam flinched. He'd been in the middle of a dream about Jake Wise. He flinched a lot when Jake was around.

"Kids, wake up," the conductor barked in a gruff voice. It wasn't Mr. Mancoso, who usually punched their tickets. It was a conductor Sam had never seen before: white goatee, twisty mustache, beady eyes. Something about him looked familiar.

"This is your stop." The conductor smiled and winked. "Better hustle."

His smile wasn't friendly. Neither was his wink. And the look in his eyes was *not* one of peace on earth, goodwill to all.

"Thank you." Sam was polite, yet as eager to get away from this stranger as he was to be off the train, in his own room, and out of his black uniform.

He urged his sister to her feet with a quick shove.

"Watch it," Leesha huffed, smoothing her clothes (a similar uniform, with a blackwatch plaid skirt and black knee socks).

They grabbed their traveling bags and leaped to the platform. The doors *whooshed* shut behind them. No one else had gotten off the train.

"That's odd," Sam mumbled, noticing how deserted the station appeared. The platform usually overflowed with people, coming and going. *Maybe everyone went home early for the holiday weekend,* he reasoned.

Stepping around snowdrifts, Sam walked toward the station. It looked the same, only different. He glanced toward the *Hollister* sign to make sure he and Leesha had gotten off at the right stop. It wasn't there.

"Hey!" he called to a worker on a ladder against the brick building. "Where's the sign?"

"Took it down for painting and repairs," the man hollered back.

Sam didn't miss the worker's resemblance to the train conductor. They could have been twin brothers, down to their white goatees.

Leesha began to pace the platform next to the parking lot. "I can't believe Cameron is late," she complained. "Father will hear about this."

"Father won't care." Sam trudged after her. "Let's walk home."

"But Cameron should be here with the car. That's what chauffeurs are supposed to do. Chauffeur you."

Sam buttoned his Woodhaven jacket to ward off the brisk wind. "So, Cameron forgot. I used to walk home all the time — before *you* came along." He started off across the parking lot. "It isn't far."

"But my bag is too heavy." Leesha's voice was whiny and annoying.

Sam made a U-turn, snatched up her bag, and started off again, leaving her to tag along, carrying the shopping bag from Dobson's.

Staying far enough ahead for the distance to mute her complaints, Sam let his gaze travel the area as he walked. Something *was* different.

But what? Houses looked the same, plump with snow on roofs and piled in yards. Christmas lights already twinkled in the dimness of late afternoon. Reindeer and Santas lay half buried in drifts from yesterday's blizzard. And the hearty smell of wood smoke flavored the air.

I'm just tired, he told himself, pausing at a corner to switch the luggage into opposite hands. Leesha's bag was much heavier than his.

She caught up with him. "Was that tree here before?" She pointed at a gigantic gold-trimmed evergeen filling the center of a large intersection.

"You, too?" Maybe he *wasn't* crazy. Maybe *she* was noticing something weird as well.

"Me, too, what?"

He lowered his voice, as if that strange conductor might be listening. "Do you get the feeling something's not quite right?"

"Yes!"

For once, they agreed on something.

"And I know what it is."

How'd she figure it out already?

"It's a *fake* tree! See the wires? It was put up for the holidays, that's all. Come on."

"Noooo. Not just the *tree*. I mean, doesn't *everything* seem . . . well, seem *off* to you?"

"Off?"

"Sort of like the earth rotated too far today? And . . . and spilled over into somebody else's tomorrow?"

"Huh?" She gaped at him as though he'd suddenly grown donkey ears.

7

"Forget it." He hurried ahead, whistling Christmas carols to take his mind off the feeling of certain doom, growing inside him like a balloon.

A balloon of doom?

The temperature seemed to dip one degree with each step closer to the Hollister mansion on Hollister Boulevard. Plus, afternoon was sliding into twilight far too early.

Sounds disappeared. No chittering squirrels, no winter crows cawing at neighborhood cats, no cars.

Even Leesha hushed *her* chittering and peered at their surroundings.

Near the mansion, they followed the curved wall circling manicured grounds and gardens. At the entryway, the wrought-iron gate was ajar.

Danger tapped Sam on the shoulder and pointed at the gate.

"I know, I know," he mumbled. The gate was *never* left open. They always had to ring a buzzer and identify themselves. Even Cameron had to holler a password at the speaker before the gate slid open for the Hollister limo.

Sam and Leesha exchanged hesitant frowns.

Maybe someone accidentally tripped the hidden switch that released the lock from the inside. *Oh, well.* Sam nudged the gate open with an elbow, and they started up the drive.

Behind them, the gate clanged shut, echoing loudly in the silent afternoon.

Ice-trimmed trees hid Sam's view of the mansion. A sense of foreboding lay draped over the mini-forest like artificial flock on Christmas trees.

Leesha began to run toward the veranda.

"Wait!" Sam called. Why was she in such a hurry?

He trotted after her, suddenly glad he didn't have to deal with this bizarreness alone.

Leesha waited by the double oak doors.

Sam could tell by the wide-eyed look on her face that she'd changed her mind about dashing inside alone.

"Hurry up," she whispered.

Why was she whispering?

Plopping the bags down on a welcome mat in the shape of the *Run for Your Life* game board, Sam reached for the solid gold door knocker. It was shaped like this: $.

His hand trembled as he let the knocker bang against the gold plate.

Then he held his breath.

He knew — they *both* knew — something was terribly, terribly wrong.

2.
Welcome Home

A tiny door at eye level opened. An eyeball peeked out.

Before it closed, Sam heard a voice exclaim, "It's young Master Samuel and Miss Leesha!"

"Whew!" Leesha stammered. Relief flooded color back into her face. "That was Cameron."

The balloon of doom in Sam's chest began to deflate.

Cameron. He *always* answered the door. That's what butlers did — when they weren't acting as chauffeurs.

The normality of the scene made Sam chuckle. Why had he felt so unsettled all the way from the train station?

The door creaked open.

Slowly.

Inside, the foyer was dark.

Sam wondered why the lights were off.

He and Leesha stepped over the threshold. The

traveling bags were whisked out of Sam's hands as the door slammed shut.

Blinking, he waited for his eyes to adjust.

The foyer and staircase were decorated with burning candles and lights. Ah, Christmas decorations. That explained the dimness. Pretty ordinary — except for one thing. All the candles and lights were . . . black!

Sam twirled. "Cameron, what's — ?"

Leesha gasped, staring at the butler. "W-what is that thing sticking out of his n-neck?" she sputtered.

"And why is his head square?" Sam sputtered back.

"Welcome home, children." Cameron, who seemed a foot or two taller than he'd been at Thanksgiving, gave a deep bow.

It sounds *like Cameron*, Sam's mind told him. *But it looks like . . . like Frankenstein!*

Plomp!

Leesha fainted.

Sam dropped to his knees beside her while Cameron called for Emma.

"Wake up, Leesh!" He wanted to add, *Don't leave me alone with this monster!* But he didn't want to insult the butler, who acted as if nothing was out of the ordinary.

"Emma, bring smelling salts!" Cameron hollered.

11

Seconds slipped into minutes before Sam heard Emma coming down the hallway from the kitchen. "What's taking her so long?" he grumbled.

Slowly Emma appeared, walking with a shuffle. Sam wondered if they'd woken her. As she drew closer, candlelight lit her face.

Sam couldn't take his eyes off her. Emma's face was paler than death. Her lips, blood-red. Her hair, usually worn in a tidy knot on top of her head, was loose, flowing, and unkempt. Her vacant eyes stared straight ahead, and her uniform was tattered.

Emma stooped, sluggishly swirling the salts under Leesha's nose.

Coughing, Leesha shoved Emma's hand away, opening her eyes as she raised herself up on one elbow.

Sam wanted to warn her, but what could he say? *Don't worry about Emma. She seems to be in a zombie trance this afternoon?*

"Yikes!" Leesha cried, scooting away from the maid. "Sammy, what's happening?"

Before he could answer, Leesha screamed, "Mummy! I want my mummy!" Then she scrambled to her feet.

Cameron bowed. "I will ring for your mum, and take your bags to your rooms." He tugged twice on a rope cord by the door, lifted the bags as though they were empty, and headed up the curved marble staircase.

Meanwhile, Emma was slow-trudging her way back to the kitchen. She hadn't spoken a word.

Leesha gaped at Sam. "What's *happened* to them?"

"I don't know. Let's ask Mother."

"Where are my darlings?" came their mother's voice from the front parlor.

Leesha dashed toward the room.

Sam followed, suddenly believing the adage about safety in numbers.

"Mummy, Mummy, where are you?" Leesha wailed. "Ohhhhh!"

Plomp!

Sam tried to catch her this time but he wasn't fast enough.

"How was your trip home?" asked Mother.

Only it wasn't Mother. It was a . . . well, a *mummy*. A real live mummy. If mummies *were* alive.

The voice was hers, and the eyes, too, from what Sam could see. The rest of her was wrapped in white gauze, causing her to walk with tiny steps. Some of the gauze had unwound from her head, and fluttered about her shoulders like long white hair.

"The trip was fine." Sam fought to keep his voice steady. *Play along*, he told himself. *Act normal. And wait for someone to shout, "Surprise! Did we scare you?"*

13

Then he could reply, "Oh, no. I knew all along you guys were teasing."

But his stepmother didn't shout, *"Surprise!"* Didn't even question her daughter's fainting spell.

Instead, she said, "You two run upstairs and change for dinner. Wear something Christmas-sy, like black sweaters." Then she sank into the couch and picked up the magazine she'd been reading: *Bad Housekeeping*.

That's when Sam noticed the dead Christmas tree, all decked out with black lights, black ornaments, and gaily wrapped presents scattered underneath. Gaily wrapped in black paper.

"I *hate* black," he muttered.

Then he noticed the silver cage, home to his mother's beloved pet dove, Peace. What hunched on the perch was *not* a white dove. It was a black vulture.

Sam helped Leesha to her feet, staying between her and the monster that used to be their mother, so his sister wouldn't faint again.

"Upstairs," he urged, shaking her awake and aiming her toward the foyer. "Hurry!"

They rushed through the dark foyer and up the dimly lit staircase.

"Son!" His father's voice echoed from the second-floor landing.

"Father!" Sam double-timed it up the steps. His dad would know what was going on. He knew

14

everything. He was vice president of the Hollister Corporation, maker of *Run for Your Life*.

"Wait for me!" Leesha began to take the steps two at a time.

"Are you home early from work?" Sam called.

"No, I'm home for the holidays, just like you two."

Sam and Leesha hit the landing out of breath. "Father," Sam huffed. "What on earth — ?"

That's all Sam got out before the glow of black lights woven around dead boughs on the banister offered him a good look at his father.

Samuel M. Hollister (the second) stood tall, wrapped in a black cape. Sam's first thought was that he overdressed for dinner. Then Sam noticed his dad's ears. Had they always been pointed? Or had he just gotten a bad haircut?

And why was his face so pale?

With a quick swoop of the cape, Father spread his arms. "Come children," he beckoned. "Give your ol' father a great big, welcome-home hug."

He grinned. Sharp fangs glimmered in the eerie candlelight.

Somewhere in the dark, Sam could hear Leesha hyperventilating.

Plomp!

This time, Leesha was *not* the one who fainted.

15

3.
Guess Who's Coming to Dinner?

Sam lay on Leesha's frilly mauve bed quilt, recovering from his nightmare. Nightmare — ha! It wasn't night and he wasn't dreaming.

Leesha slumped in an overstuffed chair by the window. The mauve chair matched the quilt, the mauve shutters, mauve carpet, and the mauve paint swirls decorating the wallpaper.

Mauve was Leesha's favorite color. Sam hated it.

The color reminded him of the creamed rhubarb Emma always tried to get him to eat. Yuck!

The odd thing about Leesha's room was that it, too, had been decorated with black Christmas lights. So had his room, the bathroom they shared, and every room and hallway he'd been in so far.

Why had Cameron and Emma decorated the *entire* house with Christmas lights? Wasn't that holiday overkill?

And where were the twinkly reds and greens from years past?

16

Sam tried to focus on his reason for being in Leesha's room — to figure out why the Hollister family was experiencing a "weird attack." But his mind kept drifting.

This used to be his favorite room. The play-room. Before his father met Leesha's mother and married her.

The cool thing about the playroom was that it connected to his room via a long, narrow closet. Sam liked to think of it as his own secret passageway.

He used to Rollerblade on the hardwood floor around his room, down the hall, and around the playroom (before the mauve carpet was installed). Then he'd barrel through the closet back to his starting place.

Before Leesha and her family moved in.

For that matter, he had the whole house to himself, *and* he had Cameron and Emma and Fa-ther to himself — before Leesha and her family moved in.

"I've got it!" Leesha yelped, springing from the chair.

Sam took a deep breath and glared at her. Why give her the pleasure of knowing her unexpected shout had stopped his heart mid-beat?

"Someone has cast a wicked spell on Mummy. Well — on the others, too," she added, as though the others probably *deserved* a wicked spell.

"Creepy Tales and Magic Spells," Sam mut-

17

tered. "You got that idea from a story in our language arts book."

He and his stepsister shared classes since they were the same age. That in itself was bad enough. Adding insult to injury was knowing she and Jake Wise had taken a liking to each other. Go figure.

"This isn't some book you're reading in class, Leech. This is real life."

"Don't call me Leech; it's disgusting."

He started to say, *You're disgusting*, but he did once when they were playing catch in the back garden, and she'd flung her mitt at him. It whacked him on the side of the face, and he had *mitt burn* for a solid week.

"People don't put magic spells on others." Sam sat up on the bed, stretching. "That's ridiculous."

"Then *you* come up with a logical explanation why Cameron suddenly turned into an overgrown monster. Or why Emma joined the living dead. *Or*, why Father sprouted fangs, and Mummy wrapped herself in toilet paper."

"It's not toilet paper."

"LEESHA!" A muffled shout came from the hallway.

Sam tensed to bolt for the closet passageway. Then he realized it was only Webster.

"I wanna play game!" he barked.

18

They grimaced at each other. Webster was obsessed with *Run for Your Life*. All he ever wanted to do was play the game — with them.

"You can come in," Leesha called. "But it's almost time for dinner. We'll have to play afterwards."

The door swung open and Web bounced into the room. He was a normal five-year-old: chatty, goofy, annoying, silly, hairy.

Hairy?

Sam came off the bed in one leap.

Leesha sank into the overstuffed chair.

Webster grinned at them. Tufts of reddish fur sprouted from his face and arms. His ears were puppy ears; his hands, claws. His nose was long and narrow, and his teeth, well, his teeth were sharper and pointier than you'd want your five-year-old brother to have.

Plopping the game onto Leesha's desk, Webster unfolded the board and set out the game pieces.

Leesha knelt by Web's side, gingerly reaching to touch his furry arm. "What's happened to you?" she whispered.

He lifted his nose, as if sniffing her scent. "What do you mean?"

"Ohmigosh, Sammy. He doesn't know."

"Web." Sam knelt on the boy's other side. "Is anything, um, *wrong* with you?"

"I'm *not* sick," he growled. Literally.

Webster had been a sickly toddler, so his mother hovered over him, keeping him indoors at the slightest sniffle.

"That isn't what I meant." Sam reworded his question. "Do you feel okay?"

"I'm hungry."

That's not the answer Sam wanted. He scooted away.

"Wanna play game," Webster demanded.

A bell chimed from the intercom system above the door.

"Time to dress for dinner." Leesha started to shove her little brother toward the door, then reconsidered, as if she didn't want to anger him. "Go downstairs. I promise to play the game with you later."

"Goody." Turning, Webster loped from the room.

Leesha stared after her little brother, biting her lower lip to keep the tears away. "Meet you in three minutes?" Her voice wavered. "So we can go downstairs, um, together?"

Sam would rather go out the window, and as far from the Hollister mansion as he could get. But, first of all, snow had begun to fall in fat clumps, and he couldn't think of any place he could run to. All his friends from school lived in other towns.

And, second, in spite of the storm of weirdness swirling around the house, nothing *bad* had happened. Maybe strange, bizarre, odd, peculiar, alien, and curious. But not *bad*.

"Three minutes is fine," he told her.

As he stepped into the shadowed hallway, something moved.

Jumping back into Leesha's room, he slammed the door and made a beeline for the closet. "Safer route," he mumbled to her quizzical look.

Sam hurried through the "secret passageway," and peeked into his room. The coast was clear. Relieved to be alone in familiar surroundings (except for the black lights) he dove into the rear of his closet where summer clothes were stored.

Choosing a Hawaiian shirt splattered with orange and red flowers, he paired it with rust-colored slacks. (Jeans weren't allowed at the formal Hollister dining table.)

Someone tapped at his closet door.

"Who is it?" he singsonged.

Leesha burst into his room. "Don't leave me in the dark," she hissed. "Tonight of all nights."

She wore a plaid dress in bright squares of pink, yellow, and green. Ha — she'd had the same brainstorm as he. Together, they'd brighten up a dreary dining room.

"Ready?" Sam tried the door to the hall, half expecting it to be locked. *Don't be silly*, his mind told him as the knob turned easily in his hand.

Sam and Leesha descended the stairs. As they approached the dining room, music began to play.

Music *always* played during dinner, but tonight, it should have been Christmas carols. The mournful dirge that met Sam's ears was more like funeral music.

Leesha was walking so close to him, she practically shared his shoes. Yet, at this point, he didn't care.

In the dining room, a fire crackling in the hearth was the lone homey detail. The room was decorated with dead evergreen boughs dotted with more black candles.

Sam shook his head in dismay. In this house, ever*green* seemed to mean ever*dead*.

The family gathered around the table, while Emma and Cameron stood to one side, waiting to serve. An ice carving of the wizard from *Run for Your Life* graced the center of the table.

The scene looked like a Norman Rockwell painting, only Sam didn't remember the families in Mr. Rockwell's paintings being monsters.

Cameron pulled out a chair. "For Miss Leesha," he said, flourishing one arm.

Leesha made a face at Sam, then gulped. Trudging around the table as slowly as Emma, she took her place.

Sam tried to ignore the look of disapproval in his mother's eyes when she saw what her son and daughter were wearing. Since her eyes were almost the only part of her face that showed, ignoring them was difficult.

"Master Samuel?" Cameron pulled out another chair. The one next to Father. Sam wasn't sure he wanted to sit that close to a vampire.

As he started to move, an icy hand came down on his shoulder. Chills ran through him. Slowly, he turned.

Before his eyes, a mist swirled, folding in on itself like Emma's breadmaking machine. Gradually the mist took the form of a person, shimmering in the firelight until the cloud was almost solid.

Almost.

Sam could still see the china cabinet — right through the hazy figure.

Moving closer, the *thing* bent to kiss his cheek.

The kiss was an ice cube searing his skin.

"Good evening, Samuel," a feathery voice hissed.

"G-G-G-Grandmother Hollister?" Sam rasped. "Is that you?"

4.
Slithering Soup and Sinister Sugarplums

A bell tinkled.

"Dinner is served," Cameron's voice boomed. *"Bon appétit."*

Sam dashed to the table — and away from the phantom who was his grandmother.

Taking his seat, he tried to act as if all was normal and well.

Normal and well?

Maybe if he kept saying the words over and over, they'd come true.

Cameron moved around the table, swooping napkins into laps, then tying a bib around Webster's neck.

"I'm too old for a bib," Webster mutter-growled.

Cameron patted the boy's furry head. "You say that every night."

Yeah, Sam's mind added. *But he's never bared his fangs at you before.*

Emma set a bowl of steaming soup in front of

24

Sam. The aroma was odd. He couldn't guess its origin. Even so, it was *not* an aroma that made his mouth water.

Sam stirred his soup, but his eyes stayed glued on what Emma was serving his father. A tall goblet of . . . tomato juice?

"Mmm mmm," his father exclaimed, sampling the drink. "Not too hot; not too cold. Just the right temperature — ninety-eight point six."

Sam shuddered. He glanced at Leesha. She was staring at her mother's plate. It was empty. Everything Emma tried to serve her, she waved away.

"Nothing for me, thanks," the mummy said. "Haven't been hungry for . . . goodness, for *eons.*"

Sam gulped.

Meanwhile, Cameron was serving chicken to Webster. Not too unusual, except it was the *whole* chicken — complete with feathers, head, claws, wings, and a tail.

While Sam and Leesha watched in horror, Webster snarfed down the chicken in three bites. Then he reared back his head and howled.

"No howling at the dinner table, dear," his mother told him.

Webster leaped from his chair and loped away to play.

Emma served soup to Leesha.

The sight was the most normal thing Sam had

witnessed since the dinner bell rang. Sighing, he tried to concentrate on eating, and ignore the waking nightmare playing itself out at the dinner table.

As he started to slurp his soup, it wiggled. Well, the soup itself didn't wiggle; something *in* the soup wiggled.

Sam stirred the broth. Little *things* were swimming between the noodles.

His eyes cut to Leesha. Chatting with their ghost grandma, she absently lifted the spoon to her lips. How could he warn her?

He didn't need to.

At that moment, Grandmother took her first swallow. Since she was transparent, Sam could see the soup sliding down her throat, or rather, slithering down her esophagus.

Leesha dropped the spoon, gaping at her see-through granny.

Sam locked his eyes on the dripping ice wizard centerpiece to keep from retching.

Leesha shoved her bowl away. Soup splashed over the edge and onto the tablecloth. Wigglers headed for cover under the silver butter dish.

Mother gave her a disappointed frown. "Aleesha, darling, your soup's getting away."

Leesha's answer was so high-pitched and breathy, Sam had no idea what she said. In a flash, she tore across the dining room and out the door.

Sam could hear her shoes pounding up the servants' stairway behind the kitchen.

"May I please be excused?" His voice was achingly polite. The last thing he wanted was to anger his parents. What would these monsters do to punish him? Getting a reduction in allowance suddenly seemed like no kind of punishment at all.

"Don't leave," Father commanded. "Emma prepared a special dessert for you."

Visions of sinister sugarplums danced through Sam's head.

Slumping in his chair, he tried to look exhausted. "Today's been really long," he said, faking a yawn. "Final exams, packing, the trip home. . . ." He let his voice trail off. "I'd really like to go to bed."

"Let him go, darling," Mother said. "Emma can save the creamed rhubarb for tomorrow." Her eyes sparked mysteriously. "*Tomorrow* night will be special. A real celebration."

"Hear, hear." Father raised his goblet of . . . of whatever.

"Hear, hear." Grandmother lifted a cup of tea.

Cameron chuckled, and even undead Emma seemed to react. For an instant, Sam thought he saw a glimmer of life in her eyes. Then it was gone.

Why is everyone so excited about tomorrow night?

"Oh, Emma," Mother called. "Let's make Christmas Eve dinner a traditional feast. For the children," she added, nodding toward Sam. "Roast turkey with mashed potatoes and gravy. Cranberries and marshmallow yams. Pumpkin pie and fruitcake."

Cameron bowed, answering for Emma. "As you wish, Madam Hollister."

Sam's mouth watered. What he wouldn't give to have all that right now. Pushing away from the table, he started to take a few swallows of milk to calm his empty, grumbling stomach.

On second thought, he set the glass down. Memories of migrating soup might keep him from eating for *eons*.

Slipping from his chair, he headed toward the foyer.

Cameron stopped him. "Aren't you forgetting something, young man?"

Usually he and Leesha kissed their parents good night before turning in. Boy, wasn't Leesha the lucky one?

"Good night," Sam whispered, giving his father a quick peck. His pale cheek was deathly cold, as if he'd been helping Santa at the North Pole.

Sam hurried around the table so his father couldn't return the kiss — just to be safe.

Pausing next to his mother, he aimed a kiss toward the spot where her cheek should be. The mummy wrapping was rough and smelled like an ancient Egyptian tomb.

"Don't forget me," came a raspy voice from the other end of the table. "He always forgets his old granny," she added.

Sam groaned. Just like Grandmother not to let him off the hook.

As president of the Hollister Corporation, she paid attention to detail.

Moving around the table, Sam hesitated, worrying about proper etiquette. How does one kiss a ghost?

Grandmother motioned him close, patting her pale, wrinkled cheek.

Gulping, Sam stooped to plant a quick kiss.

Plant was not the right word.

His puckered lips went right *through* his grandmother's wispy cheek. . . .

5.
Run for Your Life

S am tore upstairs, straight to Leesha's room. The door was locked.

He pounded on it. "Let me in!" He didn't want to be left alone out there in the dark hallway any more than *she* had wanted to be left alone in his closet.

Why? his mind asked. *This is your home. You've lived here all your life.*

"I don't *know* why," he argued back. "I can't even trust *soup* anymore. How do I know this hallway is safe?"

"Who is it?" Leesha singsonged, imitating him.

"You know who it is!" Why was she trying to be funny at a time like this?

When the door opened, Sam rushed inside. Webster was hunched over Leesha's desk, attempting to shuffle *Run for Your Life* playing cards.

The sight was so familiar, Sam almost convinced himself to ignore the furry claws wrapped around the cards.

Almost.

"We're starting a new game," Leesha said, taking her place at the desk. "The last game never ended; we must have done something wrong. Want to play with us?"

Sam checked to make sure she'd locked the door. "How can you sit there calmly playing a game? Weren't we just at the same dinner? Or didn't you notice the monsters?"

Leesha's gaze whisked from Sam to Webster and back three quick times. Meaning, Sam assumed, *"Watch what you say in front of the littlest monster."*

He agreed. But why? What would Webster do?

Maybe Leesha was right to sit here calmly playing the game with Web, acting as if nothing was wrong. Maybe this was the way to figure out what was *really* going on.

"Okay, deal me in."

The desk wasn't big enough for three people. (Well, two kids and a werewolf . . .) Leesha carried the board to the bed, careful not to tip off the game pieces.

The three settled in around the board while Leesha dealt cards. Webster's job was arranging game pieces, but he kept dropping them. His claws weren't meant for doing detail work.

They were meant for ripping whole chickens apart.

Sam shook his head to erase the disgusting

31

image of his little brother with chicken feathers fluttering about his snout.

Instead, he rescued game pieces from the floor and returned them to the board.

"Who do you want to be?" Web more or less barked the question.

Sam knew better than to ask for the *Werewolf* piece. Web always chose that one. "I'll be the *Skeleton* tonight."

"Sis?" Web set the *Skeleton* in the *Start* square.

"Mmm. I'll be the *Witch*," Leesha said.

"Good choice." Sam gave her a smirky grin.

Leesha iced him with one nasty look.

"I go first," Webster declared, tossing the black dice with white dots onto the board.

They always let Web go first to prevent him from pouting. Who wanted to be in the same room with a pouting werewolf?

"One, two, three . . ."

Web insisted on counting the dots each time he tossed the dice. Sam bit his tongue to keep from blurting, "SIX!"

". . . four, five, six."

The dice were shaped like pyramids with rounded corners, meaning *four* was the highest number of dots on each. And, meaning Sam never had to suffer through Web tediously counting all the way to twelve.

Webster picked up the *Werewolf* piece. Sam

thought he resembled it: reddish fur, pointy black nose, sharp teeth, bushy tail. (Yes, he even had a tail. His clothes had been altered — by Emma? — to accommodate it.)

"One, two, three . . ."

Now Webster was counting squares on the board as he moved his game piece out of the *Start* box.

He landed on a larger square marked *Parlor*. Since the real Hollister mansion was designed after the game, the drawing of the game parlor was identical to the actual parlor downstairs. (Except the game parlor didn't depict a dead Christmas tree. . . .)

The other rooms on the board also mirrored rooms in the real Hollister mansion: the nursery, den, alcove, pantry, sun porch, drawing room, playroom, and trophy room.

"I'm safe in the parlor," Webster declared, waiting for his brother or sister to prove him wrong.

"The parlor is *not* safe," Leesha said, challenging him.

They each fanned their playing cards. The back of the cards depicted the "evil wizard," who controlled the characters in the game. On the front were the various players.

The object was to draw from each other, then flip the cards over in the parlor. If Webster's card

33

held "power" over Leesha's, his game piece could stay put and take another turn. Hers had to return to *Start*.

The "order of power" was decided before each game by drawing tiny plastic "power squares" from the "power cup," and placing them in order on a tray in the middle of the board.

For this game, the order of power was:

Vampire
Witch
Frankenstein
Ghost
Werewolf
Mummy
Zombie
Skeleton

Leesha and Webster drew, flipping over the cards. Hers was the *Ghost*, his, the *Zombie*.

"*Ghost* beats *Zombie!*" Leesha cried. "Run for your life!"

Webster snatched his game piece out of the parlor and returned it to *Start*. "Rats," he mumbled.

Sam waited, heart stopped. The *normal* Web hated to be "overpowered." Would the *monster* Web do more than grumble?

"Take your turn," Webster snarled, wrinkling his wolf nose.

Sam's heart resumed beating. Monster or not,

Web *always* snarled at him when he wasn't paying attention.

The game proceeded as usual until Leesha flipped over a wild card. A wild card meant everyone had to "run for their lives" back to *Start*. Wild cards displayed the evil wizard's picture on both sides.

"Hey, *Skeleton*," Leesha said, giving Sam a nudge. "Web and I ran. You didn't."

Sam mumbled an answer as he moved the *Skeleton* back to *Start*.

But his gaze never left the wizard's face, staring at him from the upturned wild card.

Where had he seen those eyes before? And that nasty smirk that seemed to say, *"I know something you don't know . . ."*?

6.
My Zombie Nanny

Tap . . . tap . . . tap.

Sam had just declared, "I'm safe in the drawing room," when the slow tapping began. He caught Leesha's worried frown. "Are you going to answer the door?"

"I was hoping *you* would." She bit her lip, looking worried.

"*I* was hoping to bolt through the closet to my room," he answered.

Before she could argue with him, Webster sprang off the bed, and yanked open the door.

Emma's tall, thin frame filled the doorway. She aimed a bony finger at Webster, then crooked it upward, which meant, Sam assumed, "*Come with me*" in zombie talk.

"Web, it's bedtime," Leesha said, interpreting Emma's silent gesture.

"Not yet," he whined.

They went through this every night. Usually Emma held firm, hands on hips, until Webster obeyed. Sometimes she threatened to call in a higher power — mother or grandmother — before Web let her take him to the nursery and put him to bed.

"We'll play again tomorrow," Sam offered. He'd rather all higher powers stayed away tonight. Too many monsters in one room made him nervous.

"Yeah," Leesha agreed. "I'll even let you help me wrap Christmas presents."

Sam whispered, "Thought you were going to make Emma do it."

"It would take her till Easter to finish," she whispered back.

Webster reluctantly set down the *Werewolf* game piece.

Leesha kissed her brother on top of his scraggly head, then gave his neck a good rubbing, as if he were a puppy.

Web padded down the hallway after Emma.

Leesha slammed the door and heaved a sigh she must've had bottled up inside her ever since Webster had shown up.

For a moment, neither she nor Sam spoke.

Then Leesha calmly began to pack away the game. "Sammy, we can't just go to bed and pretend nothing is wrong. Can we?"

Sam had been thinking the same thing. "You're right. We need to snoop around a little." He tried to devise a plan. "Clues *must* be hiding somewhere in the house. We've got to find them."

"But I'm afraid to go downstairs. I'm afraid to leave my room."

So was he. But *that* wasn't going to solve anything. He helped her scoop game pieces back into the box. "Let's wait until everyone's gone to bed. Then, we can sneak downstairs, and see what we can find."

"Tonight?"

"Did you have other plans?

"No, but why the hurry?"

"Because." He squinted at the ceiling, searching for the logic of his reason. It refused to show itself. "After you left the table, Mummy — er, I mean, *Mother* asked Emma to serve a feast tomorrow night, and called it a celebration. Everyone lifted glasses to toast her. It was weird."

"You're getting paranoid." Leesha stuck out her bottom lip the way she did whenever she disagreed with him. "First of all, everything that's happened since we got home from school has been weird. And second, it's Christmas Eve. We always celebrate Christmas Eve with a big dinner."

He agreed with point one, but not point two. "*My* family doesn't do Christmas the night before. I mean, we didn't before *you* guys came along. We had our feast at noon on Christmas day."

"When families combine, they compromise on holiday traditions." She sounded defensive.

"I know, but I don't think Mother was referring to Christmas when she called it a celebration."

"So, what was she referring to?"

"I don't know. But it made me nervous. If something bad's going to happen tomorrow night, I want to know about it now. I don't think my heart can take more surprises."

"Okay." Leesha popped the lid onto the game box. "We'll go sleuthing tonight. When? Midnight? The witching hour?"

Why'd she have to say that?

"Father doesn't go to bed until midnight. How about one? Or two? To be sure everyone's asleep?"

"Fine." Leesha picked up her bedside radio. (It, too, was mauve.) She twirled the dial, setting the alarm.

Sam headed toward the closet.

"Where are you going?"

"To bed. I'll meet you here at two. Wear sneakers so we don't make noise and wake any monsters."

"Don't leave." She scrunched her face at him. "I was hoping you'd sleep on the floor."

"On the floor? You mean, *here*?"

"Well, don't you think we should stick together? What if something awful happens while we're in separate rooms?"

He'd had the same thought, only he wasn't going to let her treat him as though she were in charge. "Great idea," he told her. "Why don't *you* sleep on the floor in *my* room?"

She folded her arms, insulted by such a suggestion.

"Then we'll go back to Plan A. See you dark and early. Good night."

" 'Night," she said, giving in.

Sam fought his way through Leesha's clothes until he came to his closet door. Getting through the passageway had been easier when this side of the closet was empty. Now it was filled to capacity. She had more clothes than he'd owned since birth.

Stepping into his room was eerie. The small bedside lamp lit one corner. Misshapen shadows cast by the tiny black lights claimed the rest.

Shadows that seemed to slip and wiggle into place the instant he looked at them.

If soup could slither, then shadows could, too. With the mysterious law of slithering in the Hollister mansion, anything could wiggle.

Feeling unsettled, Sam made sure the door to the hall was still locked. Then he searched his dresser for the mini-flashlight Cameron had given him before his camping trip with Woodhaven's Outdoor Education Club.

Cameron. Sam always liked Cameron. Still did, he guessed. Even with metal bolts sticking out of his neck. . . .

Clicking on the flashlight, Sam knelt to shine it under the bed. Looked pretty normal: Rollerblades, hockey stick, hidden Christmas presents, dust. He searched behind and under every piece of furniture — twice in the closet — before being certain he was alone.

Setting his alarm for two A.M., Sam changed into his *Run for Your Life* pajamas. Grandmother Hollister had licensed the game characters. Now the Hollister Corporation released tie-in products every year.

In Sam's room alone were *Run for Your Life* sunglasses, mug, poster, pencil set (featuring a different monster on each eraser tip), book covers, and a comb and brush set.

Sometimes Sam wished his grandfather had never invented the game. Why couldn't Samuel M. Hollister the first be famous for inventing something normal? Like pizza.

He immediately pictured himself wearing pizza pajamas decorated with tiny pepperonis. Ugh. Maybe pizza wasn't such a great alternative.

Climbing into bed, Sam reached to click off the lamp. On second thought, he left it on, pulling a pillow over his head to block the light.

As he dozed, music drifted to his ears. *Oh, Christmas tree, oh Christmas tree, thy candles shine out brightly.*

Christmas carols, Sam's sleepy mind told him. *Someone must have turned off that dreadful dinner music.*

He smiled at the *candles shine out brightly* line. Black candles didn't reflect light as brightly as white —

Sam burst out of bed. The pillow went flying. That normal sounding music was coming from *outside* the mansion.

Carolers!

If Cameron welcomed neighborhood carolers into the Hollister mansion, his family's terrible secret would be tomorrow's banner headline in the *Hollister Gazette*:

Famous Family Turns Into Horrible Monsters!

The Hollister name would be ruined. No one would buy the game anymore. The company would fold. The family fortune would dwindle to nothing. No more boarding school, limos, butlers, or nannies.

Poor Grandfather Hollister would roll over in his grave! (Which was all right with Sam as long as he *stayed* there . . .)

With a panicked gasp, Sam realized what he must do.

His family's reputation in the community — in the *world* — rested solely upon his shoulders.

He had to stop the carolers.

7.
We Wish You a Miserable Christmas

S am fumbled with his bedroom door, forgetting it was locked.

In the hall, he bolted for the stairs, practically sliding down the slick marble steps on his bottom. He hit the foyer the same moment Cameron arrived to greet carolers with a tray of holiday treats.

Three frantic NOTS exploded in Sam's mind at the same instant:

1. Cameron could NOT open the door and stand there for all the carolers to see.

2. Cameron could NOT invite neighbors and townspeople inside the Hollister mansion to view the dead Christmas tree with its black lights and candles.

3. Cameron could NOT serve the carolers whatever was on his tray. What if the snacks crawled into people's hands? Yikes!

"Stop!" Sam yelped as the butler placed a gloved hand on the door latch.

Cameron faced him, a stunned look on his square face. Candlelight flickered menacingly off the crude stitches sewn across his forehead. "But Master Sam, the knocker has sounded. We have guests."

"Let *me* answer the door."

Cameron drew back, appalled. "This is highly irregular. Answering the bell is *my* job — since long before you were born."

"Hot cocoa," Sam blurted, thinking fast. "There's none on your tray. Go back to the kitchen and ask Emma to make some."

The butler hesitated.

"We *always* offer hot cocoa to carolers," Sam reasoned.

Cameron locked eyes with him for a second, then bowed, placing the tray on a sideboard. "As you wish, young man." His tone made it clear he didn't like taking orders from his boss's grandson. "Hot cocoa, coming up." He disappeared down the hall toward Emma's kitchen.

Sam yanked open the heavy oak door and slipped out to the veranda. It was then he realized what he was wearing.

Pajamas decorated with vampires, zombies, werewolves, and all the other game monsters.

The singing stopped.

A half-dozen carolers, bundled against the wintry chill, stared at him.

Sam cleared his throat. "Please go away," he said, shivering in the frigid air. "My family is . . . well, they are out of sorts tonight."

Quick thinking, his mind told him.

"Are they ill?" came a concerned voice. "Do they need help?"

"Where's Cameron?" someone else asked. "Is he sick, too?"

"No," Sam blurted. "They aren't sick. They're just, well, they're not themselves tonight." He groaned at the truthfulness of his words. "All they really need is peace and quiet."

No one moved. Probably because in past years the doors of the Hollister mansion were thrown open to carolers, who loved sampling Emma's homemade fruitcake, plum pudding, and cherry pie.

Not tonight. Tonight Emma probably made *brute*cake, *scum* pudding, and *hairy* pie.

"Please go?" Sam pleaded.

Grumbling, the carolers turned and shuffled down the walk. One figure left the group, and sauntered back to the veranda.

"Nice pj's," came a sarcastic voice. "Cutesy, cutesy."

Sam recognized the sarcasm. Jake Wise. The sixth-grade wise guy. One of the three wise men in the Christmas pageant to Sam's lowly ox. He felt sure Jake had gotten the part simply because of his name.

Rats, rats, rats.

Why does he have to see me in these stupid pajamas?

When school resumed in January, Jake would blab to everyone at Woodhaven about Sam's *cutesy cutesy pj's.*

Jake was bundled from head to toe to ward off the December storm. The only thing recognizable about him was his Woodhaven jacket.

He thrust a gift at Sam. "Give this to your sister." The package was wrapped in paper from the Sunday comics section of the *Hollister Gazette.* It looked lumpy and tattered. Jake must have wrapped it himself.

"Gee," Sam gushed with fake concern. "I don't have anything for you."

Jake snickered. "Have a miserable Christmas."

Sam answered by slipping inside and slamming the door.

Right now he didn't have time to anticipate what kind of misery his cutesy pj's would cause back at school.

Not when his numb toes were frozen to the floor.

And not when Frankenstein was barreling toward him with a tray of steaming cocoa — and no carolers waiting in the foyer to welcome.

46

8.
Werewolf Melody

Sam couldn't sleep. He kicked off the quilt, then pulled it on again.

He rolled onto his side. His chest. His back.

His stomach rumbled from hunger, but he refused to go downstairs for a midnight snack.

What if *he* turned out to be someone *else's* midnight snack?

The thought made him shudder.

His body begged for sleep, but his mind stayed wired. Asleep, he was vulnerable. Awake, he had a chance.

A chance for what?

To escape if someone comes after me.

No one's come after you yet. Not even Cameron, although he was clearly irritated at you for scaring off the carolers.

Sam laughed out loud at his conscience. "*I* didn't scare off the carolers. I *asked* them to leave. If

I'd wanted to scare them, I'd have let Frankenstein open the door."

On second thought, it would've been great fun to see a terrified Jake Wise fleeing in horror.

Sam rubbed his hands together. Maybe he could arrange a meeting between Jake and the monsters. He'd send a brief note inviting Jake over, and sign the note: *Love, Leesha.* . . .

Stop, his mind told him.

Sam glanced at Jake's gift. His curiosity tempted him to open it, but fear of Leesha's possibly painful retaliation made him leave it alone.

Arf, arf, arf. Arf, arf, arf.

Sam woke, confusion stumbling through his brain. A dog on the radio was singing "Jingle Bells."

The numbers 2:00 blinked at him in neon blue.

"It's time," he whispered, wishing it was time to race downstairs and open Christmas presents instead of time to figure out what — or who — had cast some wicked, wicked spell upon his family.

He only hoped he could break the spell — and live to tell about it.

Getting dressed was pointless. Sneakers on, trusty flashlight in hand, he stole through the closet and tapped on Leesha's door.

She was fully clothed in matching mauve

sweats, with *Woodhaven* sewn across the front in fancy plaid letters. Her hair was tied to one side with a poofy band (also mauve).

Girls. Sam gave his head a disgusted shake.

She aimed her flashlight into his face. "Ready?"

He shoved it away. "As ready as I'll ever be."

Leesha unlocked her bedroom door. They tiptoed into the hall. "Where should we start?" she whispered.

Sam paused outside Webster's door. Strange wails echoed from the room. Howls and growls. Moans and groans. It sounded like a litter of sleeping wolf pups caught in mutual nightmares.

A werewolf melody.

Sam watched Leesha's eyes, reflected in the ever-twinkly banister lights. "Let's start downstairs, as far from Web's room as we can get."

She was quick to agree.

He followed her down the curve of steps, pausing on the landing to study the life-sized, bronze game piece. One of each monster was scattered about the mansion. This was the Ghost.

When Sam was young, Emma had to escort him up the stairs to the nursery so he didn't have to pass the Ghost by himself. He knew it was only a statue, yet it terrified him to be near it.

Years had gone by since the sight of the phantom had bothered him, but tonight he felt compelled to stop and study it. Maybe his present fear reminded him of his earlier panic.

"Come on," Leesha urged.

Slowly they toured the first floor, weaving in and out of the pantry, kitchen, drawing room, parlor, sun porch, and trophy room.

The trophy room was unbelievable. In the past fifty years, Grandmother Hollister had traveled the world, promoting *Run for Your Life*, and ordering games made in materials and patterns from other cultures.

The room was filled with editions of the game in gold, silver, bronze, jade, pewter, and wicker. In colors ranging from deep greens and blues to bright reds and oranges, plus versions of brocade, paisley, silk, rope, denim, and even good ol' plastic.

The games varied in size, from mini-monsters to the life-sized versions hiding in unexpected places throughout the house — like the ghost on the landing.

Sam usually found the trophy room awesome. Tonight, he found it petrifying.

"Do you feel it?" Leesha whispered.

The room seemed to buzz with electricity, as if a simple spark of static might cause zillions of game monsters to spring to life. The hair on the back of Sam's neck had already sprung to life in warning.

"Mmm," he answered, wandering among display tables. Suddenly he felt hundreds of eyes piercing his skin. Were all the monsters in all the games watching him? *Yikes.*

"Let's get out of here." Gingerly he picked up a jade Mummy. It felt warm, slippery.

So slippery, it fell right out of his hand onto the jade game board. The crash echoed throughout the quiet room as loudly as if he'd dropped a two-thousand-pound jade walrus.

Sam set it upright and dashed for the door.

Leesha was two steps behind him. "That room always gives me the creeps." She scouted the area, her ponytail flipping from side to side. "What is it we're looking for?" She sounded impatient.

"Clues."

"So, what do clues look like?"

"Anything and everything. Except a red herring."

"Huh?"

"Forget it. Look for something out of place. Something to explain the craziness that's swallowed our family. Something unusual."

The way Leesha was sneering at him could win a prize.

Sneer of the year.

"*Everything* here is unusual," she shot back. "When was the last time you saw black Christmas lights? Or the last time your dinner ran away from you? There you go. Clues. Can I go back to bed now? I'm cold."

The ancient drafty house was always cold. Even in summer. Sam was used to it, but tonight's chill sank deeper into his bones than usual.

They wandered back to the parlor.

The vulture in the cage eyed them, as if contemplating its next meal. Sam hoped the cage door was properly fastened.

"I always love to look at the Christmas tree and presents," Leesha said wistfully. "Why'd they have to get a dead tree this year?" She touched a branch. Dry needles rained on the packages below. "Where'd they get these horrid lights?" she added. "And why are they still plugged in? It's the middle of the night."

Sam wasn't listening. He was gazing at the gigantic, gold-framed painting hanging over the fireplace. It was a picture of the scarlet-robed *Run for Your Life* wizard.

The wizard was supposed to resemble Grandfather Hollister, but Sam's memories of his grandfather were of a man with a kind, rosy face, pudgy and wrinkled.

The wizard's face was not kind, rosy, pudgy, or wrinkled. He was meant to be an evil wizard. Sam thought he looked the part.

Clicking on his flashlight, Sam let the beam play across the painting. Why had the wizard's face looked so familiar when they'd played the game earlier? And why did those beady eyes seem to be staring right at him?

"Sammy, let's go back to bed." Leesha hugged herself to get warm.

"Okay," he sighed, ready to give up. "So we failed as detectives." Shutting off the flashlight, he headed toward the foyer.

"Shouldn't we turn out the tree lights?" Leesha suggested. "Cameron must have forgotten."

"Right." Sam climbed over Christmas gifts to the far side of the tree. Packages blocked the outlet. He moved them, then took hold of the plug and started to give it a yank.

"STOP!"

Sam twirled.

A vampire stood in the doorway.

"F-Father?" Sam rasped.

"Do *not* unplug the Christmas lights."

"But — "

"*Never* unplug the Christmas lights. We leave them on," he said. "Forever."

Sam glanced at Leesha, who'd flattened herself against the nearest wall. He cleared his throat. "Did we, um, wake you?"

The vampire chuckled. He strode across the room, cape flaring out behind him. "No, you didn't wake me. I . . . well, I've become a bit of a night owl lately. I was up in the den working, and was called to come down. . . ." His voice trailed off as he glanced at the painting over the fireplace.

Called? Sam's mind echoed. *By whom?*

He followed his father's gaze to the picture. The wizard's unblinking eyes looked right at him. Wait a minute. Wasn't the wizard looking at him only moments ago from the other side of the room? Impossible.

"You two shouldn't be up at this hour," his father began. "Snooping at Christmas presents." He narrowed his eyes, shaking a finger at them.

Sam didn't correct his father's misconception. Let him think that's all they were doing. Snooping at Christmas gifts.

"I must go back to work now," the vampire said. "Soon it will be dawn and I can sleep." With a swirl of his cape, he departed.

"Whew, that was close," Sam whispered, wondering why his father had to wait until dawn to sleep.

Don't you get it? He's a vampire. . . .

Oh, right.

Sam walked toward Leesha. After every few steps, he glanced over his shoulder at the painting.

The wizard's eyes followed him. Not only followed him, they seemed to spark with energy. The same way the game pieces in the trophy room appeared to vibrate with electricity. With life.

Leesha gasped.

"What?" Sam whirled, looking to see if someone else had come into the parlor.

"For a second, I thought . . ." She stopped. "Oh, nothing. It's silly."

"*Tell* me. You thought what?"

In the dim light, Leesha's eyes became shadowed pools of fear. "For a second, I-I thought the wizard in that painting winked at me. . . ."

9.
Christmas Forever

In Sam's dream, the Hollister mansion was surrounded with carolers.

Only the carolers were *not* townspeople bundled in heavy coats.

They were skeletons.

Every one of them.

Wearing nothing but wool scarves around bony necks.

Mauve wool scarves.

And they were singing carols like *"Wreck the halls with boughs of folly,"* and *"Oh come all ye monsters."*

Jake Wise was there. King of the skeletons. Head knucklebone. He kept calling to Sam. Beckoning him to join them.

Be all that you can be. Join the skeleton carolers.

Sam came awake like a firecracker, breathing hard, as though he'd just done forty laps around the Woodhaven track. Why was he dreaming about skeletons? Maybe because he'd hardly had anything to eat since leaving school.

Resting against the pillow on his elbows, he closed his eyes. Images of the previous day played through his mind like a low-budget horror flick.

In those kind of movies, things happened that never made sense — much like what was happening right here in his own house.

Climbing out of bed, Sam stretched and yawned. A hot shower sounded great. He only wished taking a shower didn't involve leaving the safety of his room.

And breakfast? If he wanted to eat, he'd have to go downstairs to the alcove in Emma's kitchen. How could a simple thing like breakfast become a stress-filled ordeal?

Sam could hear the shower running in the bathroom between his room and Leesha's. She was up already.

While waiting his turn, he finished wrapping Christmas gifts, hoping the normality of the action would steady his nerves.

Emma always set wrapping paper, tape, and ribbons in his room before he arrived home for the holidays. This year was no exception, although he wondered how many hours it'd taken her to climb the stairs.

Kneeling, he pulled a box from under the bed. Inside were gifts, waiting to be wrapped.

Picking up the wooden dove, he admired his

own handiwork. Would his mummy mom like it? Was it too late to elongate the dove's beak, hunch its back, sharpen the claws, and paint it black to make a vulture?

No. The mother he used to know would love the dove.

Which gift wrap should he use? The shiny black paper? The textured black? Or the crinkly black? He chose crinkly.

Next, he wrapped Web's Elvis bear, hoping his little brother played with it instead of eating it.

His father's gift was a polished name plate for his desk at work. Brass on mahogany. It read: *Samuel M. Hollister II* in fancy letters.

Sam had carved the mahogany. The shop teacher at Woodhaven helped him with the brass plate and lettering.

For Cameron, Sam wrapped a new set of golf balls. The butler putted on the backyard golf course on his afternoons off.

Emma was getting a wall-hanging. The cross-stitched letters read: *Emma's Kitchen*. And Grandmother was getting a poofy pillow, made from white Swiss lace decorated with pearls and scented with her favorite perfume, *Haunted*.

Gee, how ironic.

The last gift he wrapped was Leesha's. He'd been tempted to buy her a roll of designer tape to wear over her mouth — but it didn't come in mauve.

Instead, he bought a boxed set of her favorite books. She liked kissing stories. Needless to say, he'd never read any of them, yet he hoped she'd like these. Besides, they were on sale.

After showering and dressing, Sam headed downstairs, carrying his wrapped gifts. No one was around, so he arranged them under the tree.

His father's words from last night came back to him. "Never unplug the Christmas lights. We leave them on. Forever."

Forever? Like after New Year's? Valentine's? Easter? When his friends came to his birthday party in May, would they ask why the Hollisters' dead Christmas tree was still lit up in the parlor?

Ha. If his friends walked into *this* house, they'd have *lots* more urgent questions than, *"Why is your tree still up?"*

"Oh," he'd answer. *"We believe in Christmas forever. . . ."*

Yeah, right.

Sam adjusted a string of lights. Then he took hold of the power cord. *So, what's the big deal?* he thought. *What would happen if I pulled the plug?*

Before the question had time to settle in his mind, a firm hand clamped down hard around his shoulder.

10.
Walking Waffles and Hidden Clues

Flinching, Sam dropped the cord. "Good morning, Cameron," he said, rubbing his sore shoulder.

Cameron bowed. "Likewise, Master Sam. Come now. Your breakfast is waiting in the alcove."

Sam was more than happy to hurry away from the monstrous butler.

The kitchen was one of his favorite rooms in the mansion — homey and bright, with lots of cabinets and shelves. A work island sat in the middle, with brass pots and pans hanging from a circular rack above it.

Beyond the kitchen, a sunny alcove overlooked the back gardens and golf course. This morning, both lay buried under mounds of snow.

Leesha sat at the table, sipping orange juice and picking at a plate of waffles. "You're late," she told him. "Webster and I came down together."

She looked at him as if waiting to be asked the obvious question.

"So where's Web?"

They both glanced at Emma, who was peeling potatoes so slowly, Sam wondered if they'd be cooked and mashed by dinnertime.

Dropping her voice to a whisper, Leesha said, "Emma gave him rabbit for breakfast."

Sam made a disgusted face.

"A *whole* rabbit, Sammy. He ate it in two seconds, ears and all, then howled a couple times and ran off to the playroom."

Sam poured a glass of juice. "Gee, sorry I missed that."

He lifted the lid off the food warmer. A stack of blueberry waffles remained, meaning he wouldn't have to wait for Emma to make more, or he'd die of starvation.

Why did the image of a skeleton suddenly flash through his mind? Sam blanked his thoughts and focused on breakfast.

Ah, the luscious smell of steaming waffles!

He stifled the urge to snatch them off the warmer with his bare hands, and snarf them down using Webster's uncivilized table manners.

But Leesha would be appalled. Instead, he used a server to pile his plate so high, the stack threatened to topple over.

Pouring hot maple syrup on top, he watched it dribble down the sides. Seconds before the first forkful disappeared into his mouth, he hesitated. "Is — is the food okay? I mean, have your waffles done anything odd? Like walk off the table?"

Leesha pretended to gag. "Pu-leez. I just ate three helpings. I think Mum — Mother — asked Emma to make us *normal* food instead of monster food."

"How nice of her."

Leesha frowned anytime his sarcasm was aimed at her side of the family. "What's the plan for today?" she asked, keeping her voice low.

Sam wolfed down a few bites before answering. "We search for more clues." His gaze fell on the statue in the middle of the garden. A white marble wizard ruled over the flowers and vegetables. In the summer, that is. Now, wearing a top hat of snow, he ruled over a dead garden — which somehow seemed appropriate.

"Today is Christmas Eve," Leesha said. "My favorite day of the whole year. And you want me to sneak around the house searching for clues when I don't have any idea what I'm looking for?"

"That makes two of us." He sipped his juice. "And I hope we figure it all out before the big celebration tonight — just in case *we* have anything to do with what they're celebrating."

In his mind, he pictured the two of them stuffed and basted for Christmas Eve dinner. The image made Sam shudder. He did *not* intend to leave this world as an entrée.

Leesha folded her napkin. "Sammy?" she whispered hesitantly.

"Mmmph?" (He answered with his mouth full.)

"I had the strangest dreams last night."

"Go on," he urged. (After swallowing.)

"In every dream — all night long — I was a *witch*."

"What's so strange about that?"

She smacked him on the shoulder — the one already sore, thanks to Cameron's iron grasp.

"Forget it," she huffed. "I thought it might be important. Like a clue. I'm sorry I told you." Making a beeline through the kitchen, she curved in a wide arc around Emma, as if she didn't want the maid's zombieness rubbing off on her.

Leesha's prissy movements were almost as stiff as the zombie's. Sam chuckled. Having a sister like her kept him entertained.

He chugged the rest of his orange juice. *A witch in every dream.* Ha! If the broomstick fits, ride it.

He laughed at his own pun — then choked on the juice.

A witch in every dream? Wait a minute. Hadn't *he* been a *skeleton* in all *his* dreams?

He slammed down the glass. *Clues.* These were clues! But what did they mean?

His mind surged into warp speed, trying to figure it all out.

As the reality hit him, he caught his breath.

Witch and Skeleton were two of the game pieces.

So? his mind argued. *Doesn't mean anything.*

Then chew on this, he argued back. *Those are the only two game pieces NOT walking around the Hollister mansion.*

Sam gulped. He and Leesha were the only two human candidates available for the job.

The realization shoved him from the table and made him race for the safety of his room — away from the obvious connection his mind refused to make.

11.
Gotcha!

As he raced up the stairs, Sam tore past his mother, coming down to breakfast in teeny tiny steps. On her way to sit before another empty plate.

"Good morning, Samuel." Her eyes crinkle-smiled at him.

"Morning." Sam kept moving, not wanting any contact with his stepmonster. Just to be safe.

Upstairs, he put on the brakes, letting his gaze travel to the door of his parents' room. Where was Father this morning? Sam *missed* him.

By now, Father should've asked him all sorts of questions about fall quarter at school: How he'd done in advanced math. What books he'd read. The mistakes he'd made playing soccer. And had he one-upped Jake Wise after Jake kidnapped the live hamsters from Sam's science fair project and replaced them with tiny stuffed rats?

(He'd tried, by putting glue on the bottoms of Jake's basketball shoes. But by game time the glue had dried, giving Jake better traction instead of making him stick to the floor.)

Sam tiptoed around the landing. Maybe he should have a heart-to-heart with his father. The way they used to when something was bothering him. And boy, was something bothering him now.

Sam knocked at the bedroom door.

No answer.

It wasn't shut all the way, so he shoved it open. Inside, the drapes were drawn, making the room as dark as a tomb.

Sam's flashlight was still in his pocket from last night. Clicking it on, he looped the beam around the room. The bed was empty. Ah, well, Father might be taking his morning walk — if Cameron had shoveled snow from the pathway.

As he started to leave, a faint squeal drew his attention. He aimed the flashlight toward the corner.

At first he saw nothing. Then the beam caught a slight movement.

Sam sucked in his breath. Hanging upside down from the high ceiling was a bat.

In one leap, Sam was back in the hall, slumped against the banister to still his thundering heart.

His father was a bat! Taking a nap.

A bat nap.

Flying around the landing, Sam banged on Leesha's door.

"Who is it?" Her voice sounded suspicious.

"Open up," he yelped. "It's me."

The door clicked. Leesha's eyeball appeared. "Who's me?"

Pushing into the room, he slammed the door and locked it.

"What's wrong now?" she asked. "Why are you out of breath?"

"We've got to play the game."

"We *have* been playing their game — acting normal. Acting as if nothing is wrong."

"No — I mean the *real* game. *Run for Your Life.*"

"Now?"

"Yes."

"But, I'm busy wrapping Christmas presents."

Sam strode across the room. "They can wait. If we don't play the game, there might not *be* a Christmas. For our family. For us. Forever."

Leesha blanketed the gifts with tissue paper so he couldn't see them. "Quit being so melodramatic, and tell me in plain English."

"Leesh, the answer to all of this has something to do with the game. I'm not sure what, but maybe we can figure it out if we just keep playing it."

She wrinkled her nose. "I'm *bored* with that game. Can't we play something else?"

Why'd she have to be so difficult? "Listen," he began. "You dreamt you were a witch — right?"

She stuck out her bottom lip. "Don't make fun of me again."

"I'm *not* making fun of you. *I* dreamt I was a *skeleton*."

"So?"

"A witch and a skeleton. Get it?"

"Game pieces," she answered in a dull voice. "Big deal."

"Very good." Grabbing the game off her bookshelf, he began to set it up on her desk. "Have you seen a witch and a skeleton at dinner lately?"

As his words sunk in, shock erased her mauve blusher until she was as pale as her mummy. "You mean . . . ?"

"We're next, Leesh. Christmas Eve celebration. Read between the lines."

"Oh, my." Sinking onto an empty corner of the bed, Leesha placed a hand on each cheek, as if already checking for witches' warts and wrinkles. "You're absolutely right, Sammy. Everyone in our family has turned into one of the game pieces."

He shuffled the cards. "I can't believe we didn't figure it out the second we arrived home from school."

"But they caught us off guard," she reasoned. "We weren't expecting it. Who could predict our family would turn into Grandfather Hollister's board game?"

Sam agreed. He positioned an extra chair next to the desk. I'll be right back."

Before she could question his departure, he slipped through the passageway. The sight of

Christmas presents scattered across Leesha's bed had reminded him of Jake Wise's gift.

In seconds, he returned, shoving the package at Leesha. "It's from Jake," he mumbled.

Leesha's eyes doubled in size. "It is? Should I open it now?"

He shrugged, not wanting to imply that it might be her last chance as a regular human being to open a normal Christmas gift — if Jake's gift could be deemed normal.

She tore off the Sunday comics wrapping paper. Inside was a music box. Leesha wound it up, and music began to play. "Rudolph the Red-Nosed Reindeer."

"Oh!" she squealed. "It's our song."

Sam swallowed hard to keep from laughing. "*Rudolph* is your song? Oh, how romantic."

Leesha wadded the comics into a ball and flung it at him.

He ducked, giving in to a laugh.

Turning her back, she positioned the music box in a place of honor on her bookshelf — next to her trophy from the Woodhaven Debate Club for giving the most rebuttals.

Sam thought it best to change the subject. He returned to the game. "Who do you want to be?"

"Anyone except the Witch." Leesha took a seat and scooped up the Zombie game piece.

Sam chose Frankenstein, then drew the plastic

squares determining the order of power. This time
it was:

> Ghost
> Zombie
> Frankenstein
> Mummy
> Vampire
> Werewolf
> Witch
> Skeleton

Then they began.

"I'm safe in the pantry," Sam announced, scooting Frankenstein into a room the exact duplicate of Emma's pantry.

"The pantry isn't safe," Leesha challenged.

They drew cards from each other and flipped them onto the board one at a time.

"Mummy beats Skeleton!" Leesha cried. "Run for your life!"

Sam's Frankenstein reluctantly returned to *Start*.

They played for hours. The game never ended. Each time they drew the order of power, Witch and Skeleton landed lowest on the totem pole.

And every challenge ended with "Run for your life." Neither was safe in *any* room. And if that wasn't enough, the losing card was always a Skeleton for Sam, and a Witch for Leesha.

70

Sam began to sweat. "This can't be a coincidence. It happens every time we roll the dice."

"I've got an idea." Leesha shuffled through the deck, tossing out cards here and there.

"What are you doing?"

"We're going to play the game again," she explained. "Only this time, we'll play *without* the Witch and Skeleton cards."

"Good call," Sam said, wishing he'd thought of it.

Leesha put all the Witches and Skeletons in one pile, setting them across the room on her (mauve) dresser.

Next, she removed the offending monsters from the power squares before drawing the new order. Now there were only six monsters.

Tossing the dice, she moved into the next room. "I'm safe in the nursery," she proclaimed.

"The nursery isn't safe." Sam held out his cards while she drew. Then he picked one from her.

He flipped his card onto the board. The Vampire. Vampire was at the top of the new power list. He gave her a smug look. "I automatically beat whatever card you hold."

"I hate it when that happens," Leesha mumbled.

"Vampire beats . . ." Sam paused, watching her flip the card.

His heart stalled as Leesha gasped.

A witch stared up at them from the overturned card, her face wrinkled in a *gotcha!* kind of smile.

71

12.
Time Is Running Out

BANG! BANG! BANG!

Leesha and Sam leaped from their chairs. Game pieces and cards went flying. Who was banging at the door?

"It's definitely not Emma's slow tapping," Leesha whispered. She cleared her throat. "Who is it?" Her wavery voice gave away her fear.

"PLAY GAME!"

"Webster?" Leesha glanced at Sam, acting as if she didn't know whether to feel relieved or more frightened.

Sam had already backed toward the closet, planning to make a quick exit. "He's *your* kid brother. Open the door if you dare."

"Don't be silly. He's never tried to hurt us."

BANG! BANG! BANG!

"There's always a first time," Sam muttered as Leesha opened the door.

Yes, it was only Webster. Loping into the room as he did yesterday.

"Are you okay?" Leesha asked.

"I'm hungry and I wanna play game."

How could a baby werewolf be so demanding?

Leesha tried to tell him she'd just spent the entire morning playing *Run for Your Life,* and if she was going to get his Christmas presents wrapped, and make him the chocolate-dipped strawberries he loved, she'd better get busy.

Webster *did* want his gifts wrapped, although the chocolate strawberries didn't appeal to him. Sam started to suggest a *rabbit* dipped in chocolate, then thought better of it.

Over the intercom, a bell tinkled, meaning lunch was being served on the sun porch. Webster didn't need a second invitation. He galloped, more or less, from the room.

"Wonder why he went downstairs when he's got two meat entrées right here?"

"That's *not* funny." Leesha wrung her hands. "My *poor* little brother."

"Poor little *us,* you mean." Sam began to pace. "Leesh, we've got to *do* something. Time is running out."

"Maybe *we* should run out."

"You mean, leave?" The idea sounded wonderful.

"Yes! Let's get out of here."

Sam's brain was already making travel plans. "We could pack our bags, catch the next train out of Hollister, and return to Woodhaven early."

73

"The dorms stay open over the holidays," she added. "For students who go home late, come back early, or don't go home at all."

"It's a perfect plan." He snapped his fingers to seal their decision. "Meet me in five minutes. The family's on the sun porch eating lunch. We'll slip out the front, and — "

"Five minutes?" Leesha bit her lip. "But I have to prepare my clothes for packing, and round up my curlers and hair dryer and — "

"Lee-sha!" Why did her good sense fly out the window every time it might come in handy? "We've got to get away *fast*. Throw some jeans and sweaters into your bag and let's get out of here. This could be our last chance."

"But I can't coordinate outfits that quickly."

"Think!" he whisper-shouted at her. "Which would you rather have? Unmatched clothes or a green warty face with a hook nose?"

That did the trick.

Five minutes later, the two tiptoed down the stairs, bags ready, jackets, hats, and gloves on.

Sam held his breath. A second lunch bell had rung, meaning someone in the family hadn't shown up for lunch.

Like them.

Two warnings were all you got. Then Cameron came looking for you, and you'd be in big trouble with Grandmother for being late. She was adamant about the family sharing noon and evening meals together.

They had only a matter of seconds to make it down the stairs, out the door, around the drive, and through the security gate.

Then run for their lives. Literally.

At the bottom of the stairs, they tiptoed across the foyer.

Sam grasped the gold latch and pulled the door open.

Squeeeeeaaaakkkkk!

Leesha poked him in the ribs.

"Not my fault," he hissed. "It's done that for years."

Out they ran, down the veranda steps, and along the drive.

Yes! Yes! Sam's mind shouted for joy. They were free from the dangers awaiting them tonight. Free! Dashing into the brisk wind, slipping and sliding on the icy drive was exhilarating.

Holding on to their hats, they ducked their heads against icy gusts that threatened to knock them off their feet. All they had to do was make it to the gate, push the secret release button, and —

Flommmp!

Sam reeled from the blow. What had he smashed into?

A person? Out here?

One second later, Leesha, head still bowed, smashed into him.

Enveloping them in strong arms to prevent their departure was . . . the train conductor? What was *he* doing here?

Then Sam noticed the eyes, the smirk, the twisty mustache.

This was no train conductor blocking their path.

This was the evil wizard himself. . . .

13.
They're Coming for Us

Three minutes later, Sam found himself locked in his bedroom.

A prisoner in his own home.

The train conductor-turned-wizard (or vice versa) had marched them into the mansion and up to their rooms with an iron hand that rivaled Cameron's.

For a few hours, Sam dozed, drained of energy from his overwhelming circumstances.

Now awake, he gazed out the window. Dark clouds rolled in, promising more snow. Promising a white Christmas.

A white Christmas. He should have been pleased. Yet all he wanted was a *Christmas*. White was optional.

The dark clouds also promised an early evening. An evening Sam was *not* looking forward to.

"Who *is* he?" Sam asked the window shutter. "I mean, I *know* he's the wizard, ruler of the game, power behind the monsters. But — *who is he?*"

Each member of his family had become — or been taken over by — one of the game monsters, yet no extra relatives existed who could play the part of the wizard.

Sam tried to recall any long-lost uncles who might have "gone bad."

Nope. Couldn't think of one. His father didn't have any brothers.

Could it be Grandfather Hollister? Home for the holidays? From his mausoleum?

"No!" Sam was unable to entertain such a thought. Grandfather had been kind. Funny. Generous. The game had made him a millionaire many times over. Townsfolk even joked about the M in Samuel M. Hollister, saying it stood for *millionaire.*

He'd given huge amounts of money to the city of Hollister. And to Woodhaven. A person like him would never turn wicked.

The evil man who'd arrived at the mansion this afternoon was *not* the ghost of Grandfather Hollister. Sam was sure of it.

Only one answer remained. The man was the wizard from the oil painting hanging over the fireplace in the parlor. Sam toyed with the bizarre idea. Could a picture come to life?

Or did it have something to do with the enormous amount of energy generated from hundreds, possibly *thousands*, of monster game pieces and wizard playing cards upstairs, downstairs, inside, and outside the Hollister mansion?

Had something sparked enough energy to make the painted wizard live and breathe? To give his Evilness a true taste of the power he'd known only in the game? A power he could now possess in the real world?

Sam shivered. His head whirled with horrible possibilities suggested by his colorful imagination.

If his analogy was correct, he knew what he must do. And he cringed at the enormity of the quest.

He had to stop the wizard.

If not, the entire Hollister family would spend the rest of their time on earth as monsters. And, after the wizard's purpose was served *inside* the mansion, what then?

The city of Hollister?

The wizard had obviously traveled outside the mansion.

Sam remembered the worker on the ladder at the train station. The one who looked just like the train conductor, who looked just like the wizard.

Could he duplicate himself?

Could he become mayor of Hollister?

Governor of the state? President of the country?

·

Evil wizard king of the entire world? The universe?

Sam clutched his head. "The Wizard has got to be stopped!"

He rushed to the bedroom door. Definitely locked. He peeked through the keyhole to see if a guard was stationed outside, but couldn't tell from his limited viewpoint.

Sam stole through the closet, listening at Leesha's door before tapping softly. The wizard must not have known about the link between their rooms — or else he didn't care if they reunited to worry and fret over their future as monsters.

Sam opened the door. Leesha was napping. The wrapped Christmas gifts, arranged on her desk, looked forlorn and forgotten in light of what had transpired.

Usually, gifts were first and foremost in Sam's mind on Christmas Eve.

But not today.

"Leesh." He nudged her. "Wake up."

She sat up, looking groggy. "What do you want me to do? Take out my cauldron and start practicing spells?"

"We've got to stop him."

"The wizard," she said. It was a statement, not a question. "How can we stop him if we can't get out of our rooms?"

Sam had already figured it out. "They'll come

for us later. To take us to dinner, right? Aren't we part of tonight's celebration?"

She nodded. "We'll be taken to the dining room. Then what? We can't run away again. Surely they've locked the doors and set the alarms on the grounds for the evening."

Leesha glanced out the window. "It's getting dark already. Whether we like it or not, we're stuck in the house."

Sam began to pace. "This is a big mansion," he argued. "There are lots of places to hide."

"You're forgetting one thing. My brother is a wolf. He could sniff us out in no time."

"Not if he's locked up."

"How do you propose to do that?"

Sam cracked his knuckles. "Same way I'd lock up a *real* wolf. Lure him into a trap. With meat. Or with Christmas presents."

"How? We don't have free rein of the house."

Why did she keep finding holes in all his great plans?

Over the intercom, the dinner bell rang.

Sam and Leesha grimaced at each other. From across the room, he could hear her teeth chattering.

Or was that *his* teeth?

"They're coming for us," she whispered. "Get back to your room."

Sam dashed through the passageway, falling

onto his bed the instant a key turned in the lock.

Cameron's giant frame filled the doorway. "Young Master Samuel," he said the same way he'd greeted Sam all twelve years of his life. "May I escort you to Christmas Eve dinner?"

It was a polite enough question, yet Sam knew he didn't have the option of refusing.

14.
Merry Christmas Eve

Sam and Leesha were herded downstairs and into the dining room.

The atmosphere seemed almost festive, although everything was still dead or black or both. *Festive* must have been the feeling in the air, Sam decided.

Dreary music drifted to his ears. Tonight, it *was* Christmas music — but heavy on the organs and harpsichords.

Voices around the table hushed as they appeared.

The family waited, all eyes on the two who tried to run away. They must be the major topic of dinner conversation.

"Come, children," Father said. "Take your places. We are ready to begin."

Sam hoped he meant begin *dinner*, and nothing more.

As promised, the table was spread with a traditional holiday feast. The turkey was golden brown, roasted to perfection, and didn't even have a head and claws like Webster's chicken at last night's dinner.

The table actually looked enticing. In the center, an ice carving of the Hollister mansion slow-dripped into a tray.

Sam quickly took his seat. His mouth watered as the flavor of fresh corn, beets, honey yams, and cranberries filled his senses.

Mmm. Spiced apple rings and watermelon pickles. Mashed potatoes and gravy with giblets. At least he *hoped* those brown things floating in the gravy were giblets.

Sam didn't wait for Emma to serve him; he didn't have all night. Heaping his plate high, he dug in, cautiously at first, then with growing trust.

So did Leesha, although she, too, peered suspiciously at every forkful before allowing it into her mouth.

Sam noticed the only other person eating "normal" food was Grandmother. Watching her was difficult, though. Who cared what happened to food once it was swallowed?

Mother's plate remained empty. Father sipped his . . . his tomato juice. Sam's mind refused to speculate what the thick red liquid might be.

Dinner tasted heavenly. He was almost starting to enjoy himself. As long as he *listened*, but didn't *look* at anyone, it all seemed quite normal.

Except for the comments about Webster shedding on the furniture.

Speaking of Webster, Sam kept one eye on him. The way he growl-slurped his turkey leg was nothing short of disgusting.

What bothered Sam most was that Webster seemed to be keeping an eye on him, too. Why? Was he contemplating his stepbrother as dessert? Would he prefer to eat someone who wasn't a blood relative?

Now that his stomach was full, it occurred to Sam that *everyone* seemed to be watching him. And Leesha.

What were they thinking? Part of him wanted to jump up and shout, "WHAT'S GOING ON HERE?" at the top of his lungs, then force everyone to tell their stories.

Father, how'd you suddenly become a vampire? Was it gradual? Did your fangs and ears grow a bit longer each day? Or was it sudden? Did you wake up one morning to find nothing in your closet but black tuxedos and capes?

And another part of him wished he were back at Woodhaven. Even his *worst* day at school was better than this. Any dastardly trick Jake Wise might pull suddenly seemed like kindergarten play — now that he'd guessed what the wizard was planning to do to him.

Cameron whisked away Sam's plate.

Leesha said *no* to dessert. Like always.

Saying *no* to dessert was so alien to Sam, he wondered if Leesha had arrived from some backward planet that never developed the *concept* of dessert.

"Yes, please," he said to Emma when she offered a slice of pumpkin pie with tons of whipped cream, sprinkled with nutmeg.

Sam was so pleased to find nothing on the table wiggling or writhing, he wolfed down the pie without even scrutinizing it first.

Then he made a mistake.

He asked to be excused.

"No," his mother said. "We need you here after dinner. *HE* has arrived."

All that wonderful food started hip-hopping in Sam's stomach.

He has arrived. Who else could Mother be referring to but the wizard? Sam *knew* he'd arrived because his Wickedness had personally escorted Sam to his prison-bedroom.

Moaning, he clutched his stomach.

Leesha's face grew as pale and wispy as Grandmother's. "W-w-who has arrived?" she stammered.

"You'll find out," Mother purred. "We have a little surprise for you two."

"Emma, can I help carry plates to the kitchen?" Sam offered.

His words drew frowns from around the table.

Okay, so he hadn't helped Emma carry dishes since he was Webster's age.

But he *had* to find a way out of the dining room. The room where he'd just eaten his last meal. The room where he might be doomed to sit, night after night, before an empty plate like his mother's.

Meaning, skeletons don't eat any more than mummies do.

Sam's mind whirred, searching for a reason to leave. *Think!* he yelled at himself. *Keeping your flesh depends on it.*

Leesha staggered to her feet. "I'm not feeling well. May I be excused?"

Was she fudging? Sam couldn't tell. If so, her acting was flawless.

In three steps, he was out of his seat and around the table to her side. "Are you okay?" he gushed, faking brotherly concern.

They locked gazes. Now was their chance. They were on their feet. Everyone else was sitting — except Emma, but she was no threat. Cameron was on the far side of the room, stoking the fire.

"Leesh," Sam whispered, close to her ear as a plan bloomed in his mind.

"SIT DOWN!" roared the vampire.

Sam and Leesha flinched, recoiling from their father.

"Do as I say." His voice returned to its formal tone.

Leesha sank into her chair.

Sam trudged around the table to sit. *Foiled again.* Now what?

"Oh, Cameron," Father called, acting as if nothing odd had just happened.

The butler set the fire poker back in its place, and moved to the table.

"We must prepare for our . . . uh . . . Hollister family celebration."

Sam closed his eyes.

He was doomed.

Silently, he willed his chair to swallow him. He'd do *anything* to get out of here.

"The time has come," the vampire added. "Finally, finally, after all these years."

He and Mother exchanged misty glances. "Go, Cameron," Father ordered. "Go and fetch the wizard."

15.
The Transformation Celebration

No one spoke.

Sam stared over the top of the centerpiece at Leesha's scared face.

Her soon-to-be-green-and-ugly face.

Leesha's lower lip quivered.

Sam felt like crying, too, but what good would *that* do? The evil wizard didn't strike him as one who'd give in to hysterical weeping and pleading.

Sam would save weeping and pleading as a last resort.

The only sound in the room was the crackling of the fire.

And an occasional whine-growl from Webster, who was having a horrible time sitting still and waiting. It wasn't in the nature of a five-year-old boy *or* wolf to sit still. Putting the two together made it doubly hard.

Sam felt as squirmy as Web. *You can't sit here*

and let the inevitable happen, his mind warned.

Then YOU *think of something*, he argued back. *I'm tired of coming up with all the plans.*

We're the same person.

I know that.

Somewhere a door slammed. Footsteps echoed in the silence of the family's anticipation.

Sam waited for his life to flash before his eyes.

You're not going to die. You're simply going to be transformed. Into a skeleton. That's all.

Same thing.

No, it's not. You'll still be able to think . . . won't you?

With what? I won't have a brain. Just an empty skull. No heart. No liver. No spleen.

"Stop it," Sam mumbled to his inner voice.

All eyes turned to watch the wizard stride with confidence into the dining room. He was dressed in a scarlet robe. The same one he wore in the painting over the fireplace.

"Good evening, Ghost, Vampire, Mummy, and friends."

Why isn't he using real names?

Sam knew the answer before his mind had time to express it: *Because he's got power over my family. It's no longer* Mr. Hollister, *the man who used to have power over him. It's* Vampire, *who now reports to the wizard.*

"All preparations are final," the wizard an-

90

nounced. "We are ready to begin. Please follow me to the trophy room."

Leesha wrinkled her lip at Sam. She must be thinking the same thing as he: *Not the trophy room.*

Everyone rose from the table, following single file behind the wizard's flaring robe. Mother was having a great deal of difficulty making Webster calm down and walk like a well-behaved werewolf.

Father and Cameron sandwiched Sam and Leesha between them, preventing the two from fleeing.

"Father," Sam whispered, keeping his voice low so the wizard wouldn't hear. "Help us."

Maybe if he tried hard enough, his words could reach inside the vampire and find the part of him that was still his father. The part who wouldn't want his own flesh and bone to become bone and bone.

Father looked at him. Sam couldn't read the expression on his pale face.

"Please?" Sam whispered. "Help me stop the wizard. I'll turn you back into my father, Samuel Hollister. Then we'll reclaim Mother. And Grandmother. Web and Cameron and Emma."

His father's death-white features turned dreamy, as if he vaguely remembered the names Sam was listing. From long ago and far away.

"You don't want to be a vampire, do you?" Sam whispered.

"I-I . . ." His father shook his head.

"Then, help me — "

Cameron whisked Sam around to his other side. Away from his father.

"Cameron?" Leesha whispered, continuing what Sam had started. "You don't want to be Frankenstein, do you?"

"With all due respect, Miss Leesha," the butler said. "Kindly shut up."

The procession wove its way down hallways, through many rooms and alcoves, then up a short flight of stairs to the trophy room. Emma took an extra five minutes to catch up with the others, but she finally joined them.

The room was dark, lit only by small lamps. Eight of them. Each a crystal-ball bulb held up by one of the game pieces. The light reflected off countless monsters filling the room, casting troops of larger-than-life silhouettes across the walls.

Memorabilia in front of a curved bay window had been moved aside to make room for a table covered with a black cloth. The wizard took his place behind the table.

The Hollister family gathered in a half circle as the wizard poked candles onto spiky holders and lit them.

Raising his head, he took in the audience. "Welcome." A wicked smile spread across his face, making his mustache curl up at the corners. "Tonight," he proclaimed, "the game will be complete."

Applause skittered through the small crowd. (Only those with hands actually clapped.)

"Let us begin." The wizard narrowed his eyes, focusing on Sam. "Step forward, lad."

Lad. He's not using my name, either — because names have power.

Sam didn't move. "My name is Sam," he said. "Samuel M. Hollister the third, son of Samuel M. Hollister the second, who is standing on your right and grandson of Samuel M. Hollister the first, WHO CREATED YOU!"

By the end of the sentence, Sam was screaming.

The wizard's eyes grew wider with every name. "Do not speak unless I demand it!" he shouted back.

"HOLLISTER, HOLLISTER, HOLLISTER, HOLL — "

"SILENCE!"

The glass in the bay window rattled.

The wizard took a deep breath, and leaned his hands onto the table to calm himself. "Now, lad. Step forward as I ordered."

Sam had no intention of moving, yet his feet came off the floor. He flew through the air, settling down again in front of the table. "Thank you, Cameron," he muttered. "That will be all."

Leesha actually had nerve enough to snicker.

One glare from the wizard stopped her. "You must wait your turn."

Ha, Sam thought. *As if she was in a hurry to become Witch Leesha.*

The wizard picked up a flask. Holding it to the candlelight, he swirled the liquid. A variety of small bottles were perched on the table. He chose one, adding a few drops of its contents to the flask, swirling and sniffing it. Apparently satisfied, he placed the flask in front of Sam.

Did the wizard expect him to drink the mystery fluid? Then watch his own flesh fall from his bones until he looked like one of the game skeletons who stared at him from every corner of the room?

Except *he* would be a walking, talking skeleton. Maybe he'd be their leader. With an entire army of skeletons at his command. Cool.

Sam, get real. It's not cool.

I know that.

He also knew his and Leesha's only chance was to make a run for it.

But, at this point, how could he get the message to her? If they didn't run at the same instant, it wouldn't work. They needed the element of surprise in their favor. A double getaway surprise.

"Lad," the wizard barked.

Sam groaned. "Yes, lowly game card that Grandfather Hollister invented?"

Lightning and thunder exploded in the room at

the same time. Sam was blown off his feet, and dumped onto his behind.

So was Leesha.

"Guess I touched a nerve," he mumbled, getting up and dusting himself off.

"You will speak only when asked for a response," the wizard snarled through clenched teeth. "Then you will answer *'Yes, Mighty Wizard.'* Do you understand?"

Sam refused to answer.

"DO YOU UNDERSTAND?" The *mighty* wizard narrowed his eyes. "Fine, lad. We'll see who has the last laugh."

Holding up the flask again, he whispered to it.

Then he contemplated Sam. "You will drink this liquid I prepared for you. Next, you will repeat the following words over and over until I command you to stop:

> *Now the magic has begun.*
> *I will not flee; I will not run.*
> *Before tomorrow's rising sun,*
> *I will become a skeleton."*

Sam made a goofy face at the mighty one. "Huh?"

"Sammy, don't say it," Leesha blurted.

Cameron's hand clamped over Leesha's mouth.

His hand was so huge, it pretty much covered her entire face.

You've run out of time, Sam's mind warned.

Thanks for pointing that out.

His brain scanned possibilities so rapidly, his head ached. It was now or never. Be brave, or risk living in Bone City for the rest of his days.

"M-May I say good-bye to my sister? Aleesha Jane Hollister?" Now that Sam knew names bothered the wizard, he was determined to use them every chance he got.

"She'll still be your sister," the wizard jeered.

"But — but it won't be the same." Sam glanced at Leesha, acting as though she was his best friend. "Just a brief good-bye?"

The wizard paced behind the table, annoyed. "Do it. But be quick about it."

Cameron escorted Leesha to the victim's circle. Her eyes were two big question marks.

Please get what I'm about to do! his brain screamed at her brain.

"Hurry!" The force of the wizard's shout toppled a few game pieces.

Sam stared at his sister. "We are safe in the trophy room." He spoke each word as though weights were tied around the letters.

Leesha tilted her head, confused. "The trophy room isn't safe," she answered, playing along.

Holding her gaze, he responded on cue: "Skeleton and Witch beat Wizard."

For a heartbeat, the world stopped turning. Then, the recognition Sam hoped for burst across Leesha's face.

"RUN FOR YOUR LIFE!" she screamed.

And so they did.

16.
An Army of Monsters

S am and Leesha bolted for the hallway.
Ducking into a nearby guest bath, they locked the door behind them, and headed through the adjoining guest room.

Bursting into the next hall — they came face-to-face with a zombie.

Sam's heart dropped to his knees. Leesha began to whimper. How could — ?

In the dim Christmas lights, Sam realized the zombie was only a bronze statue.

Aggravated by the delay, he pulled Leesha into a shadowed alcove. Without an escape plan, they'd end up running in circles until captured.

"Let's split up," he huffed, breathless from fear. "Find an unlocked door or window; we've got to get *out* of the mansion. Meet me at the front gate. I know how to open it."

The fact that it was snowing heavily and they were without jackets or boots seemed a minor irritation to what they'd faced moments before.

"Let's — "

"Shh!" Leesha shoved Sam deeper into the shadows seconds before someone flew past.

He wasn't sure which monster was in pursuit. But it appeared to be — green? As in jade? Had the monsters in the trophy room joined the chase? If so, they were doomed. They could never escape an entire *legion* of monsters.

"Let's go for it," he whispered. "Meet you outside. *Soon.*" Pausing, he squeezed Leesha's arm to reassure her — but mostly to reassure himself that everything would be all right.

Lunging for the servants' stairway, he took the narrow stairs two at a time. Running footsteps echoed somewhere in the darkness.

Sam froze on the landing. This landing was the home of a witch statue. He squeezed behind the bronze form, thankful it wasn't a skeleton or he'd be visible between the bones.

Two monsters whizzed past, heading downstairs. Had they checked the second story and decided the runaways weren't there? Then it was the right direction to be headed.

As he started to slip out, three more forms flew past. Going *upstairs*. "Rats," Sam mumbled, staying where he was. Maybe he should remain hunched behind the witch forever.

A gust of wind hit his face. Flapping wings broke the silence. Sam opened his eyes, afraid to look. A bat landed on the witch's shoulder, spying on him with beady eyes.

"F-Father?" Sam hissed. "Is it you?"

The bat let out a high-pitched squeal. From somewhere in the mansion came bursts of fluttering wings. A flock of bats? On their way to capture him?

He didn't wait to find out.

In three steps, he cleared the second floor and dashed into his room.

"Safe," he panted, hurrying to the window. "I'm safe in my bedroom." With one easy twist, the lock gave way. The window slid effortlessly open. Icy air threw his breath away. *Take your jacket or you'll freeze to death. Take one for Leesha, too.*

Dashing to the closet, he riffled through his clothes for jackets.

"Your bedroom is *not* safe," came a grumbly voice from deep behind his Woodhaven shirts.

Leaping back, Sam flung the door shut.

But not quickly enough.

Something jammed between the wall and door to keep it from closing.

A wand. A wizard's magic wand.

The door burst open, banging against the wall.

"Repeat after me!" the wizard shouted, continuing the transformation celebration without missing a beat.

Holding the wand high in one hand, he thrust the bubbly flask into Sam's face with the other hand, and snarled.

"Now the magic has begun. . . ."

17.
The Wizard's
Magic Wand

Lunging toward the window, Sam flew out headfirst, eating a mouthful of snow as he slid across the ledge.

Clutching a railing that bordered the second story, he pulled himself to his feet, slipping and sliding around the landing as he stooped to keep from bumping his head on the slanted eaves.

Behind him, a furious wizard leaned out the window, whirling the wand in the air and scream-chanting words that didn't make sense.

Whether or not the words made sense to Sam, he was *sure* they meant something to the wizard. Something important and powerful. Words made magic by the wand, shooting off fire like a Fourth-of-July sparkler.

Sam scuttled around a corner before the wizard could accomplish whatever spell he was trying to cast.

Working his way around the ledge, Sam stopped beneath a gable to catch his breath. His lungs ached from the subzero air. Snowflakes stung his eyes — or were they tears?

Tears for his family and the life he once knew.

Were they gone forever? Was he doomed to remain a prisoner in the Hollister mansion? Celebrating some strange black Christmas that never ended?

Up ahead was Leesha's bedroom window. Sam scrambled toward it and peeked inside.

Leesha was cornered between the door and the bed. By a werewolf.

Sam hoped it was Webster, and not another game piece, ordered by the wizard to stalk them. *Webster* she might be able to barter with.

Tapping on the window, he caught her attention.

Her eyes froze wide. Then she nodded. The movement was slight, but he noticed it. Unfortunately, she was shaking her head *No* instead of nodding *Yes*.

Still, Sam felt he could help. *He* wasn't afraid of their little wolf brother. Not *too* much, anyway.

He tested the window. It moved with his touch. Leesha must have unlocked it before Webster arrived to stop her.

Silently, he slid the window open. Should he climb in? Or wait until she could dash out?

"Leesh," he whispered.

Now her head was whipping back and forth without any subtlety at all.

"Run!" she cried.

Sam was confused. "Not without you!" he yelled. If *he* got away, *she'd* still wake up tomorrow as a witch. Then he'd have no family at all.

Leaning into the room, he ignored the fangs Web bared in his direction. He ignored the nasty growling and the warning swipe of the werewolf's claws.

Leesha thrust both hands over Webster's head, palms forward, as if trying to push Sam back through the window from clear across the room.

Whooosh!

Sam was lifted like a cat by the scruff of his neck. His body flew through the window, coming down hard on his feet.

"Heh, heh, heh," came Cameron's monster laugh as he sneered at the prize he'd caught.

"Downstairs," he ordered. "Both of you."

"I tried to warn you," Leesha stammered as Cameron forced them out the door.

Sam felt like kicking himself. Why hadn't he realized Leesha and Webster weren't alone?

The wizard waited at the top of the staircase. "Good work, Frankenstein," he said. "Take them to the parlor. That room holds the greatest power."

He smiled menacingly as they passed. "This time, dear children, escape will be quite impossible."

18.
Monster Power

Sam and Leesha descended the curved stairway as though they were walking to their doom — which, in fact, they were.

"When I saw you with Webster," Sam whispered, "I thought I could get you away from him." He glanced at her terror-streaked face. "I mean, how could he hurt you? You're his big sister."

"I'd *almost* gotten away. We'd just made a deal."

Sam was enthralled. "You made a deal with a werewolf?"

She dropped her voice. "He agreed to let me go if I promised to leave the vulture's cage unhooked so he could have a midnight snack. He can't unhook the latch with his claws."

"Ewww." One bite and the pet vulture would be history.

She responded to the sick look on his face with one of her own. "He tried to talk me into taking the vulture out and handing it to him since he's too short to reach the cage. But, I couldn't do that. I told him to pull up a chair to stand on."

Sam actually felt sorry for the vulture. "Then what happened?"

"Cameron showed up before I could get out the window. I shouldn't have gone back for my jacket."

Sam bit his tongue before making any snide comments. How could he? He'd done the same thing.

The game doesn't say, "Run for your jacket, then run for your life." Remember that next time.

"Thank you," Sam muttered to his conscience, doubting there would *be* a next time.

At the foot of the stairs, Cameron and the wizard steered Sam and Leesha toward the parlor.

The Hollister family waited.

Think, Sam. You've run out of chances.

Cameron deposited them in the middle of the room, then stationed himself behind the two.

Sam's eyes cut to the vulture's cage. Two steps to his left and he could yank open the door. Would it create a distraction? Yes, but then what?

The wizard waited while the vampire and mummy (aka Father and Mother) set up the table with the black cloth in front of the Christmas tree.

The Christmas tree. As Sam gazed at it, the wizard's words came back to him. The power is greatest in the parlor. Why? Because of the tree?

Or the lights.

He thought of the buzzing vibrations in the trophy room.

Electricity.

Christmas lights. Strung throughout the entire house.

In every room, the black lights quivered and hummed.

Power.

The power was in the lights.

The Hollister mansion had always been plagued with chronic electrical problems caused by ancient wiring: overloaded currents, blown fuses, power surges.

Sam recalled one surge that blew out so many appliances, Grandmother had commented, *"That* jolt was powerful enough to bring Frankenstein to life."

Or a wizard, his mind added. A wizard who already possessed power over all the other game monsters. Is that what had caused all this?

"Never turn off the Christmas lights," his father had told him. "We leave them on. *Forever."*

Suddenly his father's use of the word *forever* made sense to him.

Forever lights. Forever power. The wizard's evil power. Forever.

Now Sam knew what he must do.

You already tried *to turn off the lights. Twice. And failed.*

Sometimes Sam wished his inner voice would take a long vacation and leave him alone.

Now his choices were down to one. He *had* to unplug the Christmas lights — or turn into a skeleton trying.

19.
Now or Never

Sam nudged Leesha so hard he almost knocked her over.

She didn't complain. Instead, she awarded him with her full attention, as if she knew as well as he that their luck had run out.

"Do what Webster asked you to do," he whispered.

"NO TALKING!" screamed the wizard.

"The second part, too."

Cameron whisked them apart, separating the two by six feet.

Opportunity refused to smile on them. Now Sam was closer to the vulture cage instead of Leesha, and she was closer to the tree.

It was too late to change the plan now. They'd simply have to work around the obstacles.

The vampire and mummy finished setting black candles, flasks, and bottles on the table. They took their places in the half circle behind the soon-to-be monsters.

The wizard pointed his wand toward Leesha. "Maybe we should start with the young lady this time."

But Leesha's eyes stayed on Sam. Waiting for his signal.

Cameron moved forward to *persuade* her to step to the table.

As much as Sam's curiosity wanted to hear the wizard's transformation poem for Leesha — especially what words he chose to rhyme with *witch* — he knew it was now or never.

"NOW!" he hollered.

Leesha lunged past him, threw open the wire door of the bird cage, grasped the shrieking vulture, and flung it toward Webster.

"No!" screamed the mummy.

"No!" bellowed the wizard.

In the confusion that followed, Sam charged the tree, diving under the branches. Slipping and swimming over Christmas packages, he grasped the light cord with both hands.

"NOOOOO!" shrieked the entire room. Even the walls reverberated the word.

Sam felt Cameron grasp his legs to wrench him away from the tree.

He held on to the cord with all his might.

Cameron yanked.

Sam didn't let go.

With a violent spark and a snap, the plug pulled free.

110

As the room exploded in darkness, a wail unlike Sam had ever heard — even in his darkest nightmares — ricocheted through the parlor, bouncing off every wall and shaking the very foundation of Grandfather Hollister's prized mansion.

20.
Chasing Peace

Sam didn't know how long he lay on the floor. The last thing he remembered seeing was a fiery comet spiraling toward the mantel above the fireplace.

"Sam, get up. We caught her."

His mother's voice made him roll over and open his eyes, blinking in the early morning light filtering through white sheers over the parlor windows.

She, meaning his mother, his *real* step-mother — not the mummy, stood by the vulture's cage holding her beautiful snow-white dove.

"I don't know how Peace got out of her cage, but Webster caught her."

Web, wearing his *Run for Your Life* pajamas and his wolf-head slippers, gazed up at the dove. He didn't even look hungry.

Then Sam noticed the tree. It was green and living. The fragrant smell of evergreen embraced the room.

Christmas lights sparkled in reds and greens and blues and golds. Not one was black.

Father strode into the room, wearing a white bathrobe.

The sight of his father — minus the bat ears and fangs *and* wearing white — made Sam feel positively giddy.

"You kids are getting us up a bit early to open presents," Father said. "But since it's our first Christmas together as a family, I guess it's all right. Besides," he crooked an eyebrow at Sam. "You were making such a racket down here. What on earth were you doing?"

"I-I . . ." Sam came to his knees, dazed and flustered.

"Chasing Peace," Leesha said, answering for him.

Sam glanced at his stepsister, amused by the double meaning of her words. She huddled on the sofa, looking disheveled. First time he'd ever seen her perfectly combed hair messed up.

Mother whisked the dove back into the cage and latched the door. "Aleesha, darling, look at you. Your slippers don't even match your robe. Are you feeling okay?"

Sam let out the sigh of relief he'd been holding for two very long days. Things were back to normal. *Boy*, were they back to normal.

That's when he noticed what he was wearing. His bathrobe with the Woodhaven logo on it. Mmm.

One worry still clouded his mind. Although afraid to look at the painting over the fireplace, he knew he must. Standing, Sam forced himself to face the mantel.

The wizard, in his scarlet robe, gazed down at him. His cheeks were pink and rosy. The white goatee and twisty mustache perfectly matched Grandfather Hollister's.

Yet, the eyes were *still* not kind. Those were *not* the eyes of his grandfather.

Then Sam remembered. The Hollister Corporation had voted to make the wizard look unfriendly, or they couldn't advertise him as *evil*.

It was a marketing decision.

Yet, what force in the mansion had given power to the wizard? An unexpected power surge, or the sheer number of game pieces? Maybe it was time to donate a few dozen games to museums around the world. Sam would suggest it to Grandmother first chance he got.

A bell tinkled.

Cameron stood in the doorway. His face was no longer square and scarred. No bolts extended from the sides of his neck.

"If you'd care to have breakfast before opening Christmas gifts," he said with a bow, "Emma has prepared a splendid holiday brunch."

"Wonderful idea," Father told him. "Shall we?"

Mother looped one arm through Father's and the other through Sam's as they headed toward the dining room. "I can't wait to open your gift," she whispered. "Aleesha told me it's something wonderful."

Sam shrugged, feeling embarrassed and pleased at the same time.

Grandmother greeted them in the dining room. She looked as solid and substantial as the chair on which she sat.

Emma fluttered about, pouring coffee and chattering a million words a second as she always did.

Sam felt like hugging them both.

He dropped back to talk with Leesha. "Did I imagine all — ?"

"No. It really happened. Trust me." Leesha's eyes flickered with mischief. "Why else would I be standing here with messy hair and unmatched clothes?"

He laughed.

"Merry Christmas, Sammy."

"Merry Christmas." The sentimental greeting sounded ordinary, yet wonderful to Sam's ears.

This year, the Hollister family Christmas had been a real howl.

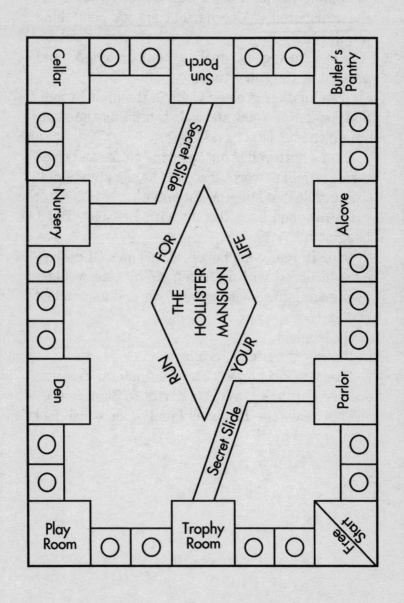

About the Author

Dian Curtis Regan is the author of many books for young readers, including *My Zombie Valentine* and *The Vampire Who Came for Christmas*. A native of Colorado Springs, Ms. Regan graduated from the University of Colorado, and presently lives in Edmond, Oklahoma, where she shares an office with her cat, Poco. Her favorite holiday is Christmas, and her favorite relatives are monsters.

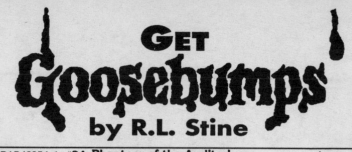

GET Goosebumps
by R.L. Stine